UNRULY DEFENDERS MC

UNRULY DEFENDER

By Esther E. Schmidt

Unruly Defender is a standalone story inspired by Vi Keeland and Penelope Ward's Cocky Bastard. It's published as part of the Cocky Hero Club world, a series of original works, written by various authors, and inspired by Keeland and Ward's New York Times bestselling series.

UNRULY DEFENDERS MC

Cover design by:
Esther E. Schmidt

Editor #1:
Christi Durbin

Editor #2:
Virginia Tesi Carey

Cover Model:
Daniel Korsten

Photographer:
Male Models Netherlands

UNRULY DEFENDERS MC

Dedication

To MY Eddy

CHAPTER ONE

EDDIE

My first intake of breath as a free man, and I'm using it to chuckle. I need another gulp of air to release a curse or two before I can manage a proper greeting. "Chancey boy, you made it."

I shake my head and stalk over to my old cellmate, Chance Bateman, who is standing next to his girl, Aubrey. A shiny car sits behind them, but it's the custom-made bike in front of the car that catches my full attention.

"And I can't believe you actually managed to do it," I tell the man as I give him a casual hug.

He smacks my back twice before stepping away so the both of us can admire the bike. It's the shovelhead custom bobber my father owned before he died. Only a week before he left this Earth he wrecked the damn thing and put it in a shed to have it fixed at a later time. There was too much going on with the club and his company that needed his attention.

I would have fixed it for him but as the new president my attention was pulled in every direction as it was. A few weeks before I ended up in jail my father stepped down and handed me the gavel to lead the MC. He didn't give me an exact reason, only that it was time. Three days after I took the gavel, he died in what the authorities ruled an accident.

But in my opinion the circumstances alone were an indication it was anything but an accident. Add the text I received a few hours before the accident, how he needed to talk to me about Rush, and the incidents after his death…everything to me seems like he was murdered and yet I have no evidence to prove my suspicions.

At least I got to bury him before I went to jail. And that's just it, my head was too clouded with the loss of my father and dealing with club business and my father's company while taking care of my mother who was devastated by the loss of her husband.

I should have seen the backstabbing betrayal coming, but I didn't. It won't happen again; I can tell you that. There will be no next time for those who killed my father and put me in jail, just so they could open roads for their own benefit and take what belonged to me and my family.

"We rushed over here as soon as I received your message. You didn't leave us a big timeframe to get here, but I'm glad you're out early. Good behavior, 'eh? I should have known. And the bike? You're a good bloke, Eddie, I figured I owed you one. I've been in your shoes, remember? Standing outside these prison walls wearing the same clothes as the day you went in." Our gazes connect and the both of us share a moment.

Yeah, he knows what it was like inside the walls of the building behind us, and how it feels to walk back out. To be thrown back into the world where everything is fucked up and you have nothing but the same old clothes on your back and a mess you left behind to deal with.

Chance smacks my back again. "It really wasn't that hard to track down your father's bike because you mentioned the address. The old man who bought it was happy I wanted to take the piece of junk off his hands. He bought it for his son who didn't want to fix it in the first place. Look at it, not so much a piece of junk now, right, mate? I made sure it was up and running so I could surprise you with it. How else were you going to get home?"

Before I was thrown in jail my mother told me someone sold my father's bike. She didn't know if it was done intentionally or by accident, but it was gone nonetheless. Right before I was locked up, I tracked down the address of the one who bought my father's old bike. I had the address but no one I could trust to head out and buy it for me.

I couldn't ask my mother and risk her being pulled into club business. They already killed my father and set me up. I mentioned it to Chance once and he seemed to have remembered the address and bought the bike back for me and fixed the damn thing on top of it.

"I can't tell you how much this means to me. What

do I owe you?" I croak, emotions getting the better of me.

Must be due to my release after years of rotting in this place for something I didn't do. I know, prisons are filled with innocent people. Those who claim to be, and those who really are. I'm not a saint, believe me, but I am one of those people who was set up and went into this shithole as an innocent man. Needless to say, I'm walking out with a mean streak of vengeance tainting my brain.

"Don't worry about it." Chance bumps my shoulder. "Are you ready to get out of here? I remember you telling me how fucking ecstatic you'd be if you were able to walk out of this place."

The corner of my mouth twitches as I remember our final talk before he walked out as a free man. Half of our discussion was about the woman standing near the car, who is watching the two of us interact. How rude am I for ignoring her completely?

I step closer and hold out my hand. "I'm honored to finally meet you, Aubrey. I've heard quite a lot about you. I'm Eddie, Eddie Barhamer."

"Hi. Nice to meet you too. You must be relieved to

be out and able to jump on that bike and ride off. Not that I think you should leave right now, but Chance told me how you were a biker. And, you know, finally getting on a bike and all." Her cheeks turn a nice shade of red.

She's cute and I understand her awkward ramblings with us standing here while she doesn't know me at all. Well, other than some details Chance might have given her. Besides, I just walked out of prison.

I throw a grin at Chance and tell him, "She's cute, no wonder you chased her down and claimed her as yours. Doesn't matter how much groveling you had to do, 'cause the way she looks at you? I'm pretty damn sure it was worth it." I direct my attention back to his girl. "You're right, I can't wait to feel the wind on my face and the roaring of the bike vibrating underneath me while it eats up the road in front of me. And I'm actually itching to leave this place behind me."

Chance throws me the keys to the bike. I catch them with ease as he says, "Let's get some coffee at the diner a few miles from here, or would you rather head home?"

I stroll over to the bike and straddle it. "Coffee sure

sounds fine to me. Besides, I have all the free time in the world. You're the only one I contacted and who knows I'm out. I'll call my mother when I'm closer to home and have bought a new burner."

I follow them to the diner and we spend over two hours talking, mainly about the two of them. When Chance walked out of prison, he didn't think he could have a future with Aubrey because he fucked it up before he went in.

Seeing them together now shows love is worth the risk. It's openly stated in their eyes when those two look at each other. Besides, if you don't know and don't try, there won't be any love to begin with. I'm happy for the both of them and the way it all worked out.

But I'm also happy to be on the road and heading home to Newport Beach. Happy might not be the correct word. Chance mentioned I would be fucking ecstatic if I was out of prison. And I am, but it's more like I'm fucking ecstatic to be able to set my plan in motion for some good old payback. I have to be careful, though. I definitely don't want to land my ass back in jail. Especially with the possibility of not being so innocent next time.

First, I'm heading over to see my mother. She runs an estate with a few bungalows; it's in my name but that's just a technicality. She loves running it along with a handful of personnel she's hired over the years. The property is right on the beach which allows the perfect vacation setting.

I mentioned it to Chance and Aubrey, and even gave them an open invitation to spend a week or weekend there. It's the least I could do because he didn't want to hear anything about me paying him back what I owed him for perfectly fixing my father's bike.

I hope they accept and swing by soon. Well, once I have everything handled that is. I've called my mother to tell her I'm on my way and that she needed to make a bed for me to crash in for the night. I don't have to mention the fact my mother was indeed ecstatic about me crashing at the estate.

Right now, it's a safe place to allow me to gather some information I need before I put on my cut and walk into the clubhouse to claim back my rightful spot as the president of Unruly Defenders MC.

Prison or not—framed by one of my own or not—

I'm still the president. And it's time for me to show everyone exactly where they stand. Even if it means some heads are going to roll and bounce onto the damn floor. By my fist with them still breathing, or their heads detached from their bodies…one thing's for sure; justice will prevail.

But again, I'm not the one landing behind steel bars this time. No amount of revenge is worth that much. So, I have to clear my head and dive into this with my eyes wide open. That's the reason I'm going to take today to catch my breath, let my body soak in a tub, and sleep on clean sheets while eating some of my mother's cooking. I missed her cooking.

This should allow me time to gather information about what's been going on while I was inside. I have the element of surprise and I want to keep going until I've gathered enough information.

I was released early from prison so no one is expecting me back. I have to be on my toes, though. The way I was set up? I'm pretty sure the one responsible wanted me gone for good. Not to mention I have a pretty good idea who is responsible, except the motive and the evidence is lacking to tie it all together or if the asshole was acting on his own or had others to support him. This being said, it wouldn't surprise me if they tried again.

I decide to take the long road home and swing by a few stores to get some necessities. This includes a new squeaky toy for my dog, Finn. I have no clue how my little buddy is doing because I haven't seen him in years.

He's a tri merle Dachshund. I know, not typically a dog for a biker, but I don't care. I found him alongside the road, tied to a tree, a mere few months old. I couldn't leave him behind and took him home after the vet thought he was able to leave. Though, that very day I became aware the little fucker had a dirty habit and it might have been the main reason they dumped him. Thing is…Finn likes to hump everything he can sink his teeth in.

Yes, I'm aware I said teeth. The little fucker only has three legs and will wrap his one paw around something while he bites down to have a firm grip. He lost his front leg the day I saved him since the one who left him alongside the road tied his leash to a tree and Finn might have been struggling, jumping, running crazy and ended up with his paw wrapped tight in the leash. The vet couldn't save it and it had to be amputated.

My mother and I share Finn when I'm needed out of town or have to work all day, whatever. I'm just glad she was able to care for him when I was locked up. I guide my bike up to the gate of the estate and enter in the security code. I wait for the gate to open and guide my bike through as it closes behind me.

I make sure to hide my bike in the garden shed on the right. Only personnel use it, so I know it's safe from MC prying eyes if for some reason they would accidentally swing by the estate. Something they haven't done in the past, but I'm not taking any chances.

I grab the backpack I bought, filled with a few new changes of clothes and some other stuff. As I stalk into the tiny office, I expect to find my mother but instead I'm staring at a nicely shaped, curvy ass leaning over a desk. It's wrapped in a tweed pencil skirt and I'm about to look away but my eye catches a lace strip. Holy shit, she's wearing garters.

I take a step back and clear my throat. I don't even know how old this woman is or what the hell she's doing here, and I'm ogling her as if I just came out of prison and need to get my dick wet this instant.

Wait. That's exactly what's happening, though I'd also like to pin her between the desk and my body and slide that pencil skirt up. Mainly to check what kind of panties match those garters, or just to check if she is even wearing some.

The woman's body goes rigid—becoming aware someone is here by the clearing of my throat indicating that she's not alone—before she slowly rises and turns. Her long black hair has a blue glow to it and it's all pulled back in a long braid. One solitary lock of white hair stands out and it makes me wonder if it's due to missing pigmentation or if she intentionally made it white.

Her heart shaped face with almond shaped eyes is intriguing, but the color of her eyes is stunning. The word supernova comes to mind. They're a bright blue with a ring of brown woven around it. I'm staring while my jaw hits the floor—with a major hard on—lacking any words to give her.

"Can I help you?" her voice is a snap of words and lacking kindness.

She might feel entitled to act this way because she caught me ogling her ass, but it's not like I had a choice with her putting it on display.

"Where's the owner?" I bark in reply.

I know I could have been nicer but she's the one who had a snap in her voice. Her eyes narrow and I'm sure she's going to say something, but Finn rushes out from behind the desk and starts to vigorously hump my leg by curling one paw around it and digging his teeth in my jeans. I can't help but chuckle and scoop him up. I'm about to cuddle the little fucker but he's taken out of my hands by the woman standing before me.

"Finn, what did I tell you about humping?" she scolds and stalks around the desk.

She bends down and I step closer to see what she's doing behind the desk as she rattles on, "This is your humping buddy," she says and holds out a stuffed goat.

A. Stuffed. Goat. There's something really wrong with this picture and it increases when Finn snatches the goat away from the woman and cheerfully starts to hump his buddy.

The woman bounces up and gives me a fake smile.

"Sorry about that. Now, how can I help you?"

"By giving me my dog back for one. And then telling me why the hell you would give him a goat to hump."

Her eyebrows scrunch up. "Your dog? He's mine."

Right. As if. My anger starts to flare but the sound of my mother's voice makes my attention slide to the left as she rushes toward me and hugs me tight. I close my eyes for a brief moment and squeeze my arms to relish in the fact I'm standing here holding my Ma.

She's been through a lot with losing Dad and then watching her son being thrown in jail, all while keeping this estate up and running. It shows how strong she is, but I can feel her shake against me and I know she's trying to fight her tears.

"It's okay, Ma," I tell her and place a kiss on the top of her head.

My mother is a tiny woman but don't mistake her shortness for lack of feistiness.

She pats my chest as she pulls away. "Well, now it is. Are you hungry? Have you eaten?"

"I can always eat if you're making something," I chuckle and rub my belly.

My Ma's face lights up with a smile. My gaze slides to the woman behind the desk who is observing us with curious eyes.

"Oh, where are my manners? Gracy, meet Eddie, my son," Ma says as she draws the woman behind the desk into our discussion.

"Oh, he's been released early?" Gracy says and instantly puts me on edge by the surprise in her voice and the knowledge she seems to have, knowing exactly who I am as she holds out her hand. "I'm Gracelynn Lightners, but everyone calls me Gracy. It's nice to finally meet you since your mother is always raving about you."

"Yeah, right," I snap and then the name enters my brain and something clicks. "Lightners, as in Lightners Yacht Club, among other things? Any relation with the magnate? Because that name doesn't come around often. So, what the hell is a Lightners doing behind my fucking desk, working in my fucking estate, and telling me she owns my fucking dog?"

"Edgar Augustine Barhamer," my mother snaps in her 'warning for hell to pay' mom voice, and it makes me feel like I'm five years old again.

It doesn't matter if I've spent the last few years dealing with the most dangerous convicts or the fact that I'm thirty-three years old; when your mother pulls out the Ma-voice, you damn well show respect and listen to what she has to say.

I hang my head and mutter, "Sorry, Ma."

"It's not me you should apologize to. I asked Gracy to come work for me almost nine months ago when I found her on the beach. She's been a real doll and works hard. Finn was taken with her right away. She has helped me and Finn because you know how much he likes the beach and his long walks. That's why she offered to take care of him along with me, and it happened to be the best solution. And really, Eddie? Judgement coming from you? I know you're on your toes, as you should be, but Gracy isn't just an employee. I consider her a good friend of mine too."

Yeah, my Ma can really make you wish for a hole in the ground to jump in and hide. You know, because deep down everything makes sense and you know she's right. And for fuck's sake, why did she have to voice my full name in front of this chick?

A sigh rips from my throat and I glance up,

catching the chick's stunning eyes first. There's a damn smirk painting those pretty cherry colored lips before she schools her features. I narrow my eyes but wince when my mother smacks my shoulder.

"Enough already. Gracy, sweetheart, excuse us, please," Ma says as she grabs my arm and drags me off.

Can I just mention I'm glad she doesn't snatch me by my ear to drag me out of the room? And why am I letting her drag me off without giving me a chance to take my dog with me? I want my fucking dog back.

—— CHAPTER TWO ——

GRACY

"Cocky bastard," I grumble to myself and take a deep breath in an effort to calm down.

I don't care how handsome he looks with his rugged appearance. All tall and fierce along with a scruffy, hard angled jaw and gorgeous blue eyes. I bet the dark, short hair was easy to maintain in prison. I wonder if he would normally let it grow out some more on the top. It doesn't matter. The things coming from his mouth are anything but nice.

Rude, and self-absorbed. I've encountered a lot of types of guys over the years, but this kind of man?

He's the whole sex-on-heartbreaker-legs package deal. Though, the "bad boy vibe" he has going on is something my ladybits enjoy more than the "filthy rich boy attitude" of those slicks my father used to throw my way.

I'm not judging them, or the fact Eddie is a convict. To each his own. Every person has their own value in life and reasoning for being either a dick or a nice person. Though, I have to say, in my experience there's nothing more annoying than a guy removing invisible specs from his own clothes in the window while he's hitting on you.

Jeez, talk about unattractive and making less effort because they think their wallet is the way into your panties. I bet a man like Eddie couldn't care less about the cash in his pants or have the need to stroke his own ego through his reflection. He looks like a guy who owns—and calculates—every move he makes. It doesn't matter. A man is still a man and the end goal stays the same; getting into a girl's panties.

Sure, there were exceptions in my past. Those guys didn't really want to get into my panties, they used me as a steppingstone into my wallet. Well, my family's wallet. Exactly what Eddie threw in my face the second he heard my last name.

That's why I have lots of experience recognizing different types of guys. Mostly because my father used to push potential future son-in-laws—he deemed worthy—in my direction. Those were the ones I quickly classified as slicks. But those weren't the only ones he would surprise me with.

Let's just say my father functions differently and that's the reason I walked away from him and his lifestyle. To make a long story short, the final straw and the reason I left was because he arranged nightly entertainment for me—otherwise known as a quick fuck—the day of my mother's funeral.

You know, to get over the fact my mother committed suicide because my father was a cheating asshole husband who loved to wave his money, and his dick, around to get as much attention as he could get. I guess this says a lot about my point of view of men and my screwed-up past. And it didn't matter if my parents had split up a few months prior to her death either, my father was a first-class asshole, there's no other way around it.

The best thing I did was leave everything behind and just walk away. I ended up sitting on the beach where Maggie, Eddie's mother, found me. I was in tears and spilled every detail of my past up to the point where my father wanted me to screw the night away to get over the fact I just buried my mother. All while she sat beside me listening as Finn was humping Maggie's hat that had blown off her head.

The corner of my mouth twitches and I glance down to see Finn sitting right next to his stuffed goat. He's panting like crazy, his tongue lolling out due to the special attention he just gave his goat.

"Any energy left in that little body of yours?" I chuckle and squat down to pet his soft head. "Or do you want to get out of here and hit the beach before we curl onto the couch?"

Finn is the only man I need in my life. Eddie might think it's his dog but he's not getting him back. No one takes my dog, even if it used to be his. Shit. He must feel the same way. After taking care of him for almost nine months now we've grown used to our routine. Maybe I'll get Eddie a gift certificate to a shelter so he can adopt a dog. Though, I bet he won't settle, because

I won't either. I glance at my watch and see it's time to wrap up here.

I scoop Finn up and grab my purse from underneath the desk before I lock up and head out to the bungalow I share with Maggie. There are a few on this estate and when she took me in, Maggie offered me a bungalow for myself or I could have her spare bedroom. Seeing I just lost my mother and left my father, I didn't want to be alone. The spare bedroom was my choice and the reason Finn and I became a team.

The moment I stroll inside the bungalow is when I realize I forgot the fact Maggie invited her son over. There's no escape when he's standing in the living room and spins around to lock eyes with me. His narrow and in return, I narrow mine too. Then I become aware I'm the one intruding and even if he was rude to me earlier, I can be the bigger person.

I briefly close my eyes and take a deep breath before plastering a smile on my face and telling him, "Don't mind me, I'm going to change real quick and then take Finn for a stroll."

I don't wait for a reply because clearly, I couldn't care less what he thinks, I was being polite for my own, and for his mother's, sake. Dashing through the hall I turn left and set Finn down when I'm inside my room. He runs off to his blanket where another stuffed animal sits. This dog never gets tired of his humping game.

Sliding the zipper down of my tweed pencil skirt, I shimmy out of it and throw it on the bed. My shirt is off next and I balance on one foot to slip out of my high heel and then take off the other one. Bending down, I place them on the floor and straighten as I catch a glimpse of myself in the mirror. Noticing instantly Eddie is standing in the doorway getting an eyeful of my body wrapped in sexy lingerie.

"What the hell?" I gasp and quickly snatch—and slide on—the fluffy robe I have hanging next to the bathroom door.

"Don't cover yourself up on my account. I mean, you're dressed to impress anyone with a sane mind for beauty. Man, just look at those curves wrapped in lace. Shit." He rubs a hand over his face. "Never mind. I didn't follow you here to get an eyeful, just give me my dog and I'll leave you to it."

He glances around and when he notices Finn, he

shakes his head before his attention slides back to me. "What's with the harem of farm animals?"

"It's to feed his addiction, okay?" I grumble, tucking the robe closer as if it will help him un-see the goods I flashed him with earlier. "I could give him a pillow for all he cares but I had a nice deal buying secondhand stuffed animals. Finn likes to rip them apart sometimes too so it's easier to throw them out and give him a new one. Now, do you mind? I'd like to change before I take Finn for a walk."

Eddie nods and is about to turn, but he points a finger at me. "No husband, no boyfriends, and from what I've heard, no dick action. So, why the garters and sexy shit when no one is giving you the right attention?"

This little sneer he throws at me pushes the wrong buttons in my head. "It's for me. *For myself.* I'm the one seeing and enjoying it. Why the hell would a woman only have a guy as a reason to wear nice lingerie?" I snap.

His head tips to the side and a sly smile spreads across his face. Shit. It's not hard to guess his train of thoughts.

"Stop with overthinking, Eddie. It's not like that, you oversexed weirdo. I'm worth nice lace and things that make me feel good about myself. Even if no one knows or notices and it's covered up by normal clothing. I could wear granny panties and a sports bra but those wouldn't make me feel pretty or good about myself. Not that I don't wear those too, because I do. I use them if I have my period. See? Mood. My mood. Not to get myself off because of some fetish or nympho… oh, why am I even discussing this with you? Get out of my room."

He holds his hands out, palms up. "No judgement, little temptress. None whatsoever. I was just curious because with me just being released from prison and all, I might have missed out on a new trend. Good to know you're—" He lets his eyes slide over my body and I need to fist my hands to prevent from letting a shiver rock my body due to a hint of this man's attention as he licks his bottom lip before he finishes his sentence with, "Your own brand of special."

Your own brand of special. Is that an incognito way of calling me a weirdo? Why does this guy make anger flare inside me at every turn?

"Out," I snap, making Finn jump up and start to bark at Eddie.

Eddie looks crushed for a moment and weariness slides into his eyes before he gives a tight nod and spins around to stalk away. I close the door and lean against it with my forehead. What a freaking mess. And way to impress the son of the woman I consider my second mother.

It's a good thing my bedroom has a large sliding door, leading to the patio where I can walk right onto the beach. I quickly change into a bathing suit and some shorts and head out, leaving everything behind me to enjoy some quality beach time, even if it's getting late and the beach is deserted. I like it this way, and so does Finn.

It's over an hour later when I stroll back to the bungalow and see Maggie sitting on the patio. Finn rushes over and crashes in front of her feet, tired from our evening stroll. Eddie is nowhere in sight and this is actually how normal evenings go between me and Maggie; enjoying some careless free minutes just sitting here and watching the sea rock the beach.

"He's good. Deep down he's a good man. He just

doesn't trust people easily, and I don't blame him after what happened, but he should have been nicer to you," Maggie suddenly says as she's staring into the distance.

"Hey." I place my hand on her knee. "Don't worry about it. I'm sure he has a lot on his plate and he just walked out of jail after such a long time. I would be groggy too."

I better not mention the incident in my bedroom, how he received an eyeful of my sexy underwear, and called me out on it.

Maggie shakes her head. "There's more to it. I shouldn't be telling you this but I trust you, and you're like a daughter to me. And from what Eddie told me there could be some danger coming our way too. See, Eddie believes my husband's death wasn't an accident like the authorities like to think it was. I've mentioned to you I own a construction company that belonged to my husband. Eddie worked his way up to earn his place in the company. Meanwhile he branched out into other things when he started to invest and made some good business decisions. He became a silent partner, and it was the boost the construction company needed because then it started to do really well. My husband took a step back so they could oversee things and it would basically run itself by the people they hired alongside the main crew. I was thankful because my William hurt his back so he didn't have to work as hard anymore. That's also why we suspect the accident that caused his death wasn't an accident, because he shouldn't have been working at the construction site. He shouldn't have been there at all because it wasn't his part of the job anymore."

Her voice cracks and I can see in the moonlight how a tear trails a path down her cheek. I lean against her and squeeze her knee in silent support. I knew she lost her husband, William—and the fact her son was in jail—but she doesn't talk about them all that much. Other than the tiny things like how she misses them and about life being unfair.

I also know she inherited the construction company and I have found her sitting at the dining room table going over financial books more than once a month when someone named Yates brings them over for her to check.

She might be hitting the sixty mark but she's

always in full control about everything. Not only running this estate but also overseeing the construction company and the bar she owns that's located down the street.

Or maybe it was the bar along with the compound next to it that belonged to her son that she looks after. It's not like I asked to see the papers or anything. Like I said, she shares little details and I've never cared about technicalities such as ownership and money. I care about the person, not the bank account or anything else that's in their name.

"I'm right here, Maggie," I tell her. "For whatever you need."

"Thank you," she mutters and wipes away her tears as she adds, "I hope you extend that courtesy to my Eddie too, he's going to need a good friend."

"Well," I tell her and clear my throat. "A friend? Okay. But whatever he needs? I'm not so sure that's going to work out all that well. He's not my type, you know. Well, if I knew what my type was because you know I have no luck when it comes to the male species."

A snort and a chuckle leaves Maggie's lips, and it

was what I was going for; to get her out of the sadness she's wrapped in.

"You're a good person, Gracy," Maggie says with a smile in her voice.

"Maybe not that good a person, Maggie. Because I don't intend to give Eddie his dog back. Finn is mine."

Maggie's laughter fills the air and I'm wearing a big smile because the sound is warming my chest. In the time I've lived here she's basically become my second mom and we share the kind of connection where we can work together but also tell each other straight up what's bugging us or just sit together without saying anything. My life took a turn for the better the day I met her.

"That's a sound I've missed hearing," Eddie's voice breaks Maggie's laughter and I glance behind me.

He's leaning casually against the wall of the bungalow and I wonder how long he's been standing there. Eddie pushes away from the wall and strolls over to sit right next to me.

I guess I have my answer when he leans in and whispers, "Finn was never yours to own, Gracelynn.

He's mine."

My breath catches and my heart starts to run wild inside my chest. All because his hot breath and whispered words stroked my ear. Shit. Like I said, he's sex-on-heartbreaker-legs. This man probably doesn't have to do anything other than smile and women will fall at his feet with their legs spread wide.

That thought sobers me up quickly. I look him dead in the eyes and tell him, "Shared custody. If you say he's yours you should think about him first. He's been with me day in and day out for almost nine months. You can't rip him out of the steady life he's been leading."

The corner of his mouth twitches and I notice because I'm staring at his lips. "Are you sure you're talking about Finn or yourself? Because I know for a fact Finn is easy to please. As long as he has somewhere to sleep, eat, shit, and hump, he's the happiest dog on the planet."

"Such a guy comment," I mutter and shake my head.

Maggie stands. "I'm going to turn in for the night. Seeing the two of you are arguing about my dog, he's coming with me."

She scoops Finn up and stalks into the bungalow. Eddie and I can only stare after her as she closes the sliding door with a big grin on her face. Shit. Something about two dogs fighting over a bone while a third runs off with it.

Eddie groans and takes his head in his hands before he starts to rub his temples. "I know what she's trying to do, but it's not going to happen."

"Like hell am I going to let her take my dog," I grumble as I shoot a glance over my shoulder to see if she's still standing there, but Maggie isn't in sight so she did, in fact, head to her bedroom.

"No." Eddie releases a deep sigh. "She's trying to hook us up."

"What?" I gasp. "You're crazy. She said you needed a friend. Besides, I've sworn off men. All men. Except for Finn. My dog." I emphasize the last part so he knows who I'm talking about and how I'm not giving up my dog.

"Fine, we all share the dog, whatever. But just a heads-up, Gracelynn, I meant what I said, you and I? Not going to happen."

"Okay, clearly your ears aren't working properly because I just mentioned how I've sworn off all men. No need to throw out the 'not going to happen' statement again unless you're saying it to remind yourself. And seriously? You go from 'my dog' to 'we all share the dog, whatever,' in the blink of an eye? That's hardly standing your ground, more like falling back on your ass in the sand and rolling over. But you don't strike me like a guy who would roll over easily," I ramble.

He keeps staring at me for a few heartbeats until his head turns to stare into the distance. "I have a lot going on at the moment. Things that need my attention and can backfire at any time. My mother is smitten with you. I think over half the discussions we've had since I got back were about you. Finn clearly likes you, so who am I to argue? Like you said, I have to think about him and my head is already filled with other shit."

I hate the way worry weighs heavy in his words. One would think a person would walk out of prison relieved to have his sentence behind him, but the way he's acting and the words he just said—and didn't say—makes me think his burdens are just starting to build up.

This makes me bump his shoulder. "Don't worry too much. Worry clouds your brain and blocks you from seeing the easy solution within your reach. And if you need anything or if I can help in any way, let me know. I owe your mother a lot. She turned my life around when I felt like I had hit rock-bottom. Whatever she or you need, I'm there, no questions asked."

He glances back at me and holds my gaze for a few breaths. No words are exchanged and his head slowly returns to the moonlight dancing over the waves in front of us. The both of us sit in utter silence and to my surprise I find it comfortable instead of awkward.

"Do you mean it?" Eddie says as he breaks the silence.

"Sure," I tell him but then realize I should set extra boundaries in place. "But, needless to say, I won't do anything involving sexual favors."

A soft chuckle is all I get in return, along with an intense stare.

— CHAPTER THREE —

EDDIE

I know I was the one stating nothing will happen between us, but when she mentioned the no sexual favors just now, I was surprised to feel regret flowing through my veins. I'm sure it has everything to do with seeing her clad in lace and knowing how good her curvy ass and thighs look. Not to mention I've gone without sex for a few years.

I need to get laid and fix the unwanted thoughts clouding my head. It's exactly like she said; worry blocks me from seeing solutions. I keep staring at this woman. I know nothing about her and yet my mother told me a lot and not to mention I know her father all too well. I've had to deal with him in the past every now and then, and so did my father.

He's a sleazy asshole who thinks he gained a throne by marrying into money. But she seems different, or so I gather. And I do have respect for her if what she told my mother about her past is true, leaving everything behind without a single backward glance. I release another deep breath and try to let my worries flow out along with it.

"Being betrayed by those who are supposed to have your back changes everything. There's doubt at every turn and it makes you see people differently." Gracy nods but doesn't say anything, so I continue, "It also doesn't give me any reason to trust you, even if my Ma vouches for you. Your father, he's—"

"He's an asshole and I'm nothing like him," she says fiercely. "Look, you should be hesitant at trusting people because people are assholes who walk this Earth as if they own it. And in some form, they do, because it's their life. Most don't have the whole 'treat others the way you like to be treated' life motto or have their own twisted sense of 'give and receive,' but that doesn't mean you have to go through life doubting everyone."

I let her words tumble in my head and a plan starts to take shape. "I could use your help to see if a buddy of mine is loyal to me or if he's teaming up with the one I suspect wants me gone."

"How can I help?" she offers instantly, but rushes a stream of words out right after. "I don't do the whole 'dig up bones or bury a dead body,' okay? I don't know you well enough to be that kind of friend. You know, the kind that comes running with a shovel in hand at any time of day."

My head tips back and laughter rips out. "You're really something, Gracelynn," I murmur.

She stares at me intently and says, "Why do you keep calling me Gracelynn? Everyone calls me Gracy."

"I like your name." I shrug. "Why use only half when the whole package is perfect the way it is."

Even with only a hint of moonlight I can clearly see my words made her blush, and I like it. I like it a lot. Maybe more than I should.

"Cut it out," she says shyly. "And tell me what you

specifically need my help with to see if your buddy is loyal to you."

I grab my burner from my jeans and hold it in my hands. "A call. I'm thinking of luring him to the bar and seeing if he comes alone or if he brings anyone else. Or—"

"Or sends someone to kill you," she easily supplies when my words lack.

"Yeah," I groan, already hating myself for pulling her into my mess, even if all I'm asking is a phone call.

She rips the burner from my hands. "Okay, how are we going to do this? What should I say? Or how could I lure him to the bar? Will a sexy voice and the promise to get some action do it?"

Again, she manages to rip laughter from my body and I shake my head. "Nah, he's the vice president of Unruly Defenders MC. Free pussy is available at all times." Her nose wrinkles and it makes me ask, "Why the disgust ruining your gorgeous face? Is it the biker part or the free pussy part?"

"Biker part. Sex is sex and what people do in their own time is their business not mine. But the bar at the end of the street is where bikers meet a lot of the time, it's right next to the compound they hole up in. One of those bikers tried to kick Finn when he was only trying to make a new friend."

I'm trying to keep a straight face when I ask, "By trying to hump the biker's leg?"

"Well, yeah." She shrugs and it makes me chuckle.

"I guess this isn't a good time to mention I'm the president of Unruly Defenders MC, right?"

She gasps and groans right after, muttering, "Me and my big mouth."

I decide to bring the discussion we were having back to where I need it to be, and tell her, "You could tell Yates you know all about the club's betrayal and have information about his president."

Her eyebrows scrunch up. "Yates? Is he the same one who brings by the books of your mother's construction company? And seriously, you're not wrapping it up or sugarcoating it a bit? Are you sure you want to approach it that way?"

"Yeah. Yates has been keeping things running since I went inside. And I need to see with my own eyes if he comes alone or not."

"Maybe he's suspicious too, ever think of that?

Then he would bring a buddy too. Or maybe he's already in the bar with some friends because those bikers are there a lot. It doesn't make sense to question his loyalty that way," she says and I hate to admit it, but she's right.

"Any chance you have a better plan?"

"Not really," she grumbles. "But I've always been one who has to see it to believe it. You know, the whole 'see it with my own eyes' thing instead of hearing what others tell you. Then you can act on your own experience and follow what your gut tells you to do."

"So, what? Head over and observe, talk to him and see what happens? No one besides my mother and you know I'm out. Well, and my cellmate, but he isn't connected to my previous life."

She keeps staring at my face and asks, "Have you always had this short hair and scruffy jaw?"

The corner of my mouth twitches again. "No. In fact, my hair was down to my shoulders and I had a full beard. I shaved it all off once I was inside."

"So, they wouldn't exactly recognize you at first sight if you would be wearing...let's say a weird touristy shirt, shorts, and flip flops?"

"Fuck, no," I tell her. "I'd never wear something like that."

"My point." Gracy smirks and adds, "Wanna get something to drink in a biker bar and see if your buddy is there? Then I could make that call and you can see how he reacts. If he warns his buddies it's clear he's in on things, right? Facial expressions should give you enough to know if he's talking bullshit or if he's honest."

"I like the way you're thinking," I compliment, and suddenly feel good about the way this evening is going. Time to set things in motion, with a little help from my newfound friend.

We agree to leave in about two hours because that's the time when most bikers would usually head over for a beer. Or at least that's what the both of us agreed upon. She dashed off to gather some clothes for me and I kid you not, she came back with a Hawaiian button up shirt with flowers and palm trees, khaki shorts, and flip flops.

Stuff previous guests have left behind and have been dry cleaned in case people return or call our lost and found to get their stuff back. Well, in this case I'm thankful for lost and found supplying me with the disguise I need to observe.

Gracy strolls out and she's wearing a red summer dress. Her hair is down in soft waves and almost reaches her damn fine ass. She's not wearing high heels but instead there are sandals with laces wrapped around her calves.

I lean in and tell her, "You look stunning. No one is going to pay attention to me at all with you right next to me. But tell me, garters or no garters this time? And are they as flaming red as the dress?"

She shoves my chest and shakes her head. "I'm wearing sandals, Eddie, so no, no garters."

"That doesn't make sense. But, damn. So, just a red lace thong then?" I question boldly, making her eyes bulge.

The corner of my mouth twitches and it seems she draws it out of me a lot.

And I let her know, "We agreed to be friends, and with me knowing you're wearing that sexy shit to make yourself feel better…again, me being your friend and all…I can see if you're right and compliment the shit out of you to make you feel even better."

She rolls her eyes. "You made a passionate plea for yourself...but, that's a no, friend. I have a mirror and can give myself compliments, thank you very much."

"Yeah, but that's different," I quip, letting my arm sneak around her waist as we stroll down the street.

She doesn't say anything about my arm and why should she? We agreed to pretend we're a couple to stake out the bar.

"Well, if I'm ever in need of a man's opinion, I know who to call," she mutters and adds, "Not that I have your number, but you know what I mean."

"Give me your phone." I hold out my hand and she digs her phone out of her purse and I smile when I see the picture.

"See? You get it." A soft giggle slips over her lips before she adds, "You should see how some people react when they see a dachshund humping a goat. Stuffed or not, people judge at seeing even a glimpse without knowing all the details."

"So very true," I murmur while punching in my number and sending a text to make sure I have her number too.

I hand her back her phone and get ready to be

aware of every single detail around me. This bar might be owned by me but I've hardly had any work from it. It's purely an investment for me and the main reason I hired a manager years ago when I bought it, and he runs it flawlessly.

I place my hand on Gracy's lower back and guide her inside. It's crowded and I instantly recognize the three bikers sitting at a table in a corner. Yates is one of them and he's sitting next to Maxton and the one I despise is sitting across from him.

Rush. That fucker is wearing the president patch as if he's entitled to. He's not. It doesn't belong on his chest and I want nothing more than to stalk over and rip it off and let him choke on it.

Soft fingers slide over my wrist and my arm is being yanked forward. Gracy pushes her body against mine and slides an arm around my neck so she can pull me down as she whisper-hisses, "Stop staring as if you would like to rip them apart. We're here to observe and not confront." She pulls back and cups my face with both hands. "Vengeance is blinding, while justice is like karma; it will hit those who have it coming right in the face. Distance yourself, Eddie. I can see it in your eyes the way you crave to get even. You've waited so long, but you're out now, you're right here. Take your time because you have loads of it. Now focus, dammit."

I could drown in her gaze and taste her lips for decades and yet she asks me to fucking focus.

"Yes, ma'am," I croak.

"Good." Her hands slide from my face to my shoulders as she says, "Now, let me buy you a drink and I'll call your buddy so you can see how he reacts. Then we'll either head home or you can hook up with your buddy and I'll head home by myself."

"I'm not letting you walk away alone, but I can't have anyone thinking we're connected once they know who I am. It's too dangerous."

Shit. What was I thinking pulling her into this? But it was too good to pass up, I need her to make sure I can test Yates.

She rolls her eyes. "I'm a big girl, Eddie."

She steps closer to the bar and leans over to give the bartender her order. There's one guy and two chicks behind the bar and I don't recognize any of them. The guy I hired to run this bar knows exactly what it needs to make a good profit every night. He isn't cheap, but he's the best at what he does.

Gracy grabs her wallet but I've already handed the guy a twenty and tell him to keep the change. I take a seat next to Gracy and the way we're sitting, it allows me to have a clear view of Yates and the others, while Gracy is blocking their view so they don't notice me. I grab my burner and punch in Yates' number.

"Ready?" I ask and she gives me a nod.

We've talked it through before we came here and we came up with a few lines for her to make sure Yates knows this is about me and Rush. So, now is the moment of truth. Will Yates be loyal to me or will he let Rush know who he's off to meet?

Gracy takes the burner along with her drink and hits the call button. She stands and strolls to the opposite side of the room so she doesn't put any attention on me and can give Yates a reason to head out the back without any suspicion. It would look like he took a random girl with him.

I take my beer and keep it in front of my face as if I'm sipping it, and slide across the room so I'm near the bikers sitting at the table. They are way too loud, and this allows me to hear them clearly and also notice their every move. Yates' phone rings. Show-time.

He fishes it from his pants and glances at the screen before answering. "Who the fuck is this?" he growls and a few seconds later he's glancing around the bar.

I know she just told him to come to her because she has information about me, and especially the hit on his president sitting across from him. But she instructs him not to say anything to Rush.

"What are you doing, Yates?" Rush asks.

Yates' eyes land on Rush as he keeps his phone to his ear. I have a clear view of Yates and I can tell by the look he gives his president that he holds no respect for Rush. His words also don't leave anything to the imagination as he glares at Rush and says, "I'm not going to sit here and watch you guys get drunk. I have better things to do."

Yates' eyes go straight to Gracy. "Later, dick-heads," Yates snaps and stands.

"Sit down, VP," Rush barks.

Yates places a hand in the middle of the table and leans into Rush's space. "You know exactly how I feel about your insane intentions to drag this club down just because you like to powder your nose. You're not getting my vote. Not now, not ever. And no amount of beer is going to change that fucking fact."

Yates pushes away from the table and stalks straight to Gracy.

Utter fury flows through my veins when he places his hand on her upper arm and guides her to the back. My heart is slamming against my rib cage, but I need to stay put for a moment. I can't draw any attention to myself, and I would if I followed them right away.

"He's never going to be on our side, Pres," Maxton says to Rush.

"Then we strip him of his rank or make sure he has an unfortunate accident. It won't be long now, things are already set in motion, it's only a matter of days," Rush states, satisfaction evident in his voice.

The hairs on the back of my neck stand on end due to this asshole's chuckle. They start to sip their beers and fall into small talk. Time to head out back where Gracy went with Yates. A few minutes have passed and I could say the Yates I used to know wouldn't hurt a woman, but after what I went through, I doubt everyone…even Yates.

Yates and I go way back. We were both prospects around the same time. He's the VP because I needed someone I could trust when I became the president. We were working side by side together in my father's company before things went to shit and he continued running it when I was on the inside. My mother said he did very well, that's the reason I'm reaching out to him first.

And I do have the feeling I can trust him completely. His reaction just now and what he said to Rush also suggests he's solid. Stalking into the back, I take a turn and check left and right but I don't see either of them. Panic flows through me. I never should have asked Gracy to help me. What if something happened to her? I'd never forgive myself. Fuck. Ma would be pissed too.

"I said you should stay put," Gracy's says, her voice an angry snap coming from further down the hall on my left.

"And I said I'm done playing games. Now, you tell me right this fucking instant what you know or you and I will have a problem." Yates has Gracy caged between the wall and his body, his hands on each side of her head.

I see red and jog over. I grab him by the shoulder and push him back. "Leave her the fuck alone," I growl in his face.

Yates is about to go into defense mode, but his eyes narrow and he takes me in as I have my forearm pressed against his neck.

"Pres?" he asks in disbelief.

"VP," I grunt and step aside. I glance back at Gracy. "Are you okay?"

"Yeah." She gives me a timid smile. "Are you?"

I have to swallow back a chuckle, but I hear Yates snicker and ask, "Did the little curvy one really ask if you're okay? Kinda makes me wonder what she'd do if you weren't...would she kick my ass?"

"Probably," Gracy mutters.

Both me and Yates now laugh as Gracy puts her tiny fists on her hips and starts to glare at us.

"Calm down," I tell her, holding both my hands palms up but all it seems to do is throw oil on the fire because now she's narrowing her eyes at me.

"Come on, we're taking you home so Yates and I

can have a chat," I suggest.

Gracy leans forward and asks in a low voice, "Are you sure?"

Yates leans in too and adds in a fake whisper, "If he wasn't, what are you going to do about it?"

I swear I blink and Yates grunts as he doubles over.

"Did you just gut punch my VP?" I ask in awe.

"I wasn't expecting it, dammit. I didn't have the damn time to prepare and she knocked the wind right out of me. What the hell are you? Fuckin' superwoman or something?"

"Nope. I'm just Gracy, his friend." She turns to me and asks, "How about him? Is he the kind of friend you'd show garters to?"

"What garters? Why is she mentioning garters?" Yates grunts as he's rubbing his stomach.

"Come on, Gracy, it's time to take you home." I lean in next to her ear and whisper, "Yeah he is, but like hell are you ever going to show anyone else but me those garters, understood?"

Gracy snorts, "You're not the boss of me."

"Well, he is the boss of me," Yates mutters. "And I think I recognize you now…you work at Maggie's estate, don't you? I've seen you once or twice when I dropped off the books. So, that would also mean he's your boss too."

"Yeah, technically, I am the boss of both of you." I'm wearing a big grin when Gracy's eyes go wide with surprise.

"All of it is yours?" she whispers but it's not for us, it's mainly to herself because she slowly shakes her head and spins around to head out the back.

We make sure to follow her and drop her off at her bungalow before Yates follows me to mine. I have a lot to discuss and plan and none of it involves dragging my new friend in trouble along with it. Not only is it too dangerous for her, but it's dangerous for me because she already occupies every dirty thought that pops into my head.

—— CHAPTER FOUR ——

GRACY

I give the two people standing in front of my desk a brilliant smile and thank them for their stay. They say their goodbyes and leave the lobby. I honestly can say that I love working here. Maggie has done a great job making this estate a success and it shows with the happy customers.

There are hardly any problems and if there is, we'll be sure to fix it right away. Another thing I love about working here is the flexibility. By splitting the front desk work with another employee named Travis, I manage to balance my hours and not get stuck behind a desk all day, every day.

It also allows me to keep an eye on everything happening around here when I do my rounds. Normally Maggie would be the one checking up on things and walking around the estate to see if everything flows fluidly, but the last three months I've been slowly taking over.

Maggie doesn't like to talk about her health but I've been noticing how she gets tired more often and has problems with walking around the estate when the temperatures are higher. It worries me but she doesn't want to go to a doctor for a checkup.

She just waves me off and tells me she's already taking it slow and it's just because her body isn't what it used to be and it's all about getting older one day at a time. I make a mental note to mention it to Eddie the next time I see him.

Though, I have no clue when the next time will be because the last time I talked to him was when he dropped me off after we went to the bar to find Yates. That was three days ago. I've only had glimpses of him jogging down the beach and watching him punch a punching bag dangling from the ceiling of his patio.

His hands covered in white tape, body all sweaty and slick.

Yes, I have no shame, and I'm honest enough to admit I've been ogling him from afar. It's not like he or anyone else saw me do it. He's too busy working out and it's too early for anyone else to be up at that time of day.

"Now there's a sight for sore eyes," a familiar voice rumbles and it makes my head whip up from staring at the papers I was checking.

Well, not so much checking, more like mind-lessly staring at because I was mentally watching Eddie's sweaty body move in a loop of a memory I have branded in my mind.

"If I knew I was going to see your gorgeous face I would have dressed up." My gaze collides with famil-iar eyes.

They are somewhat the same as mine—a ring of brownish green flowing to blue—because he too has heterochromia iridis, a genetic condition. Black glossy hair perfectly groomed with a handsome face showing off a radiant smile. He's wearing a crisp black suit with a white button up shirt, radiating the high class he thrives in.

"Clemente," I gasp, shocked he's here because the last time I saw him was at my mother's funeral. "I could say the same thing."

His father and my mother have been friends since high school but his father left for Italy with his family right after they graduated. My mother mentioned a few times in the past how she never forgot her high school crush. A few months before my mother's death they accidentally ran into each other and became fast friends again. Since me and Clemente are of the same age, the two of us became friends too.

"Nonsense, *pasticcino*," Clemente rumbles, and I've always loved the way his voice sounds when he speaks Italian, or English for that matter with a hint of an accent. "You would even look stunning if you'd be wearing a garbage bag."

I rush over and give him a proper hug. "Stop calling me a cupcake unless you bring me some. No, on second thought, don't bring me cupcakes. I'll end up eating them and my ass is big enough as it is."

A laugh rumbles through Clemente's chest and he places a kiss on the top of my head. "That's an absolute lie, Gracy. Your ass looks fine."

"What the fuck is this?" an angry voice blares through the lobby and I instantly know it's Eddie. "Get your hands off her."

I try to step away from Clemente but he holds me tight against him. "Eddie Barhamer, I presume? You look quite different than the last photograph my uncle had on file."

"Yeah, well, I was expecting your uncle for the meeting I requested, and not someone else to represent him. Now, let go of my personnel. Gracelynn, go to your room."

"Go to my room?" I gasp, completely stunned and becoming angry and frustrated of this whole situation. I have no clue what's going on but I do know one thing. "What am I? Five? Besides, this is my friend and you're being rude."

"Do you know who your friend really is?" Eddie says through clenched teeth.

Who my friend really is? What does he mean?

"Gracy, sweetheart, we'll catch up later," Clemente says and gives me another kiss on the top of my head before he addresses Eddie. "Shall we?"

Eddie points at the office on the left and Clemente heads in that direction. Eddie stalks up to me and whisper hisses, "I thought you didn't have a boyfriend or a dick to jump on from time to time."

Another gasp leaves my mouth and I'm getting sick of his attitude. "That's none of your business," I snap.

I don't say anything else and turn on my heels and stalk to my desk. Asshole. I can't believe he avoids me for three whole days and suddenly pops up and starts to order me around. In front of a friend no less. Ugh. How embarrassing. Eddie eyes me for a moment before he disappears into the office Clemente walked into and shuts the door behind him.

I grab the phone and call Travis to see if he can replace me. There's no way I want to face Eddie when he's done with his meeting and I will call Clemente later to catch up. I wish we could have talked more but Eddie ruined it. I never had any feelings for Clemente, other than friendship, but the way Eddie whispered those words to me made me feel weird.

Travis walks in with a bounce in his step. He's the kind of guy who is always wearing a smile and when you see his face with the warm and welcoming look, and the light brown curly hair standing on end, all you can do is smile back.

He stalks around the desk and bumps my shoulder. "Where's the fire, girl?"

I point at the door and huff, "The boss is in the office and I would like to be gone before the meeting that's going on in there is done."

"Maggie?" Travis questions with scrunched eyebrows.

"If it was Maggie, I wouldn't be calling you," I grumble in frustration.

"Ah, the rugged, long lost son who got back a few days ago. Hmmm, did you notice how he always takes a run down the beach each morning and a swim in the ocean right after? And I've caught him doing this kick, punch, knee routine on a punching bag…you have to get up early for those, though. Ah, three days in and I know his routine where the man gets his sculpted abs from," Travis states and his eyebrows are now dancing seductively.

Eddie goes swimming early mornings too? Sculpted… "Travis, are you ogling your boss?"

That's my job, not his. But I can't help to tease

Travis, and already my mood changes because Travis always has this effect on people.

"Girl, any man or woman with a pair of eyes would check out that man's body. From the looks of it he did some hard work to get it in that shape, and he works hard to keep it that way, so it deserves to be ogled."

"I guess I missed the memo," I mutter and grab my stuff. "Thanks for taking over. If you need me for anything, call. I'm going to take Finn for a walk first, though."

"All good," Travis says and checks the computer for the new arrivals.

I point at a name on the screen. "Just one couple coming in today but their bungalow is all set."

"Go, go, go, Gracy. I got this." Travis ushers me out.

I pick Finn up who was sleeping on his blanket. Travis looks at Finn and I know he really wants to pet him because he loves animals, but he's also very allergic so he can't. If he did, he would be a complete mess with the sneezing and eyes watering.

Instead of taking Finn for a walk, I decide to get in my car and take a drive down to the marina.

My grandfather used to own this marina but when he died it all went to my mother. Our name is connected to shipbuilding and port logistics. We own a lot of businesses, and this marina is also where Lightners Yacht Club is located.

All of it was once founded, and some bought by my grandfather. My mother's father to be exact. My father took my mother's name when they married because it came with a status. It's what my mother used to say during some of their fights.

Those fights always used to be about my father's infidelity. They would always lead to my father saying their marriage wasn't one of love. And that would be the point where my mother would throw out how he married her for her name and the wealth attached to it.

I've heard this story over and over but my grandfather explained it to me when I was older. He bought a commercial freight and shipping company and Spencer—my father—was the CEO at the time. My grandfather thought he was a good match for his daughter seeing my mother never actually got over her crush when he left for Italy.

I remember the fighting between my parents all too

vividly. When I was younger, I used to lock myself in my room or head for the marina to visit my grandfather. At a young age I was always around this place and enjoyed spending time with my grandfather. He was the one who taught me how to sail. I love the water. Swim, sail, surf, dive, or just soak in the sun and hear it slosh against my sailboat.

That last part is what I'm going for now, to relax in the sun while touching up my tan and let my mind trail off with the sounds of the water and the marina. Finn is wearing his orange life jacket and happily humps his stuffed shark before he collapses into a peaceful sleep on his blanket next to me.

I love this boat. It's not too big, not too small, and designed perfectly for my needs. Most times I just plaster myself on the pillows like I'm doing now while I have a bottle of wine in a holder and a glass in my hand.

I'm taking tiny sips and with each one I relax a bit more and feel my frustrations ebb away. I think I'm going to sleep here tonight. There's a large double bed below and the tiny cabinets are stocked with food so I can easily whip up something if I get hungry.

I'm about to give my glass a refill and put some more sunscreen on when I hear people arguing. I place my glass in the holder before I stand to see what the fuss is about. Finn follows me as I stroll to the back of my boat and to my surprise, I see both Clemente and Eddie standing in front of my boat getting in each other's face.

"What the hell are you two doing here?" I snap. "Not to mention I came here to avoid you, Eddie. And Clemente, I texted you about meeting somewhere later this week or the next to have lunch. So, I ask again, what are you two doing here?"

They both start to ramble simultaneously. My eyes hit the sky for an instant before I shush them and point at Clemente. "You first."

Yes, I deliberately skipped Eddie because I'm still pissed at him for what he said to me.

Clemente smirks and says, "I wanted to catch up with you but Travis told me you left and mentioned you were probably at the beach. Seeing I didn't want to get sand in my shoes without knowing for sure if you were there, I located your phone through an app and saw you were at the marina. Eddie here followed me when I told him I wasn't going to honor his request. Or make that a demand, whatever, it's not going to happen."

At my mother's funeral Clemente made me add him to an app so we could see where each other was, just in case we were in trouble. At the time my mind wasn't really processing but he was genuinely concerned about me. That's why I mindlessly processed his request.

"Well, as you can see, I'm fine and I was trying to relax, but with the two of you arguing, my peace and quiet has come to an end." I direct my attention to Eddie. "Clemente wanted to catch up because I haven't seen him in a long time, as for you...what are you doing here?"

"I need to speak with you, privately," Eddie growls.

"Or you can just say it with me standing here," Clemente easily supplies. "He doesn't want you anywhere near me. Which, by the way, is pretty damn hypocritical if you ask me."

"No one is asking you," Eddie snaps.

"Between me and you, I'm the one who has all the rights to be here," Clemente says in utter calmness.

His eyes meet mine and they soften before he says, "I'm your half-brother, Gracy. I've had my suspicions since the day we met. With us having the same eyes as my father, it wasn't hard to make the connection when your mother and my father reconnected. But when I took over my father's business…it came with a lot of undisclosed secrets, including this one. I wasn't going to say anything but this asshole here thinks he can ban me from your life. But instead it's the other way around." Clemente's gaze swings sideways and his tone turns to ice as he says, "I won't have you near my sister and let you drag her into the shit you're wrapped in."

"What about the shit you're wrapped in?" Eddie fires back. "Are you going to stand here and ignore the fact you're the head of one of the biggest—"

"Shut your mouth," Clemente hisses.

My mind is boggling over the flow of information and these two idiots are going at each other as if they are the ones having issues. Okay, maybe they are, but all my mind is screaming at me is "What?" And it's too insane to be true and they are dragging away my ability to process.

"Stop it!" I scream, making Finn bark along with me as both Clemente and Eddie fall silent and stare at me.

"Hey, Finn. It's okay, little man," Eddie says and shakes his head at me. "Did you really think it was necessary to add a shark fin to his life jacket?"

"Yes," I hiss. "It came with a stuffed shark for him to hump, alright?"

The corner of his mouth twitches and his whole demeanor changes along with it. "Good to know. Can you bring him by my bungalow later tonight? He's my dog too, remember? I'll leave you guys to it, and Gracelynn...call me if you need me."

He doesn't wait for a reply but strolls away instead. A deep breath flows from my lungs and I rip my eyes away from Eddie to address Clemente. "Don't just stand there, climb on board and start explaining."

I head to the front where I left my wineglass and sit down. Taking a few sips, I grab the bottle and refill my glass. Okay, I might have thrown back the whole glass in one go but really, I need it with the little tidbit Clemente just threw at me. My half-brother. Half or not, I have a brother.

"Do you have another glass?" Clemente asks.

I wave my hand in the direction where he can get his own glass. Clemente grabs one and hisses when Finn decides to give him a warm welcome by humping his leg.

I groan and grab the stuffed animal from his blanket and wave it in front of Finn. "Come on, Finny, stuffed buddies only."

Finn happily hobbles my way and snatches the stuffed shark from my hands to give it special treatment on his blanket.

"Now I can see who the dog belongs to," Clemente grumbles. "What's the deal between you and the president of Unruly Defenders MC?"

"I don't believe that's any of your business. Please, Clemente, I think we have something more important to discuss than Eddie."

Clemente stares at me and I can see it in his eyes, he's not going to let this go.

I huff and grumble, "Fine. He's Maggie's son and was released from prison a few days ago. I've been working for Maggie ever since I left my father's house the day of my mother's funeral. I was devastated and had nowhere to go and she found me on the beach, completely upset. She offered me her home and a job. And no, there's nothing going on between me and Eddie other than him owning the estate I work in. Or so it seems, because I didn't know that little detail either until a few days ago. Eddie owns the estate, so Maggie isn't my boss, he is. Again, there's nothing going on between us. We agreed to be friends, nothing sexual. And I only agreed because Maggie told me he could use a friend."

"Smart, hooking her convict son up with money," Clemente mutters.

The wine almost sloshes over my glass as I dash up and get in his face. "You take that back. Maggie isn't like that. She's a sweet woman who was there for me when I needed someone and has been there ever since without asking for one damn thing in return. So, yes, if she asks me to be a friend to her son, who has been betrayed by those who he trusted, then yes, I sure as hell will be there for him."

Clemente doesn't seem impressed by my outburst at all. He's as calm as the sea before a storm.

"Those who betrayed him are the ones who want

him dead, Gracy. He's dangerous and wrapped in things I don't want you anywhere near. If I knew you were in trouble I would have come. You should have reached out to me or to my father. I would have opened up my home for you too." There is no warmth in his voice, a hint of anger, maybe. Though, I don't feel as if it's aimed at me, more at the circumstances he's only now became aware of.

"I couldn't think, Clemente. I wasn't in my right mind the day of the funeral. Then my father arranged some guy for me to fuck to get my mind off my mother's death and I lost it. I ran away and found myself walking down the beach until I was so tired I had to sit down. I was lucky Maggie found me when she was walking Finn."

"That piece of scum isn't your father," Clemente hisses through his teeth. "Spencer is a disgrace and shouldn't have been anywhere near you or your mother."

My shoulders sag and I take a seat between the pillows, Clemente sits down next to me. The both of us are wrapped in silence as we both sip our wine.

"The day my father heard the news about the death

of your mother is when he had his first heart attack," Clemente states and my head swings toward him but he's staring at the horizon. "As you might know your mother and my father went to the same school growing up. They were in love but our world works differently. My father wanted to escape his responsibilities and run away with your mother. My grandfather found out about their plan and instantly moved back to Italy."

"I know about the sudden move of your father, and," I gasp and do a little headcount. "You're telling me my mother was pregnant with me when your father left the US?"

"He didn't know she was pregnant at the time. If he knew, he would have found a way to get back. But in our world, we have arranged marriages to forge bonds to expand the Famiglia. He knew about the woman he needed to marry; it was arranged when he was fourteen years old. It messed up his future with your mother because when his arranged wife became of age, they would be wed. It's also the reason why I was born. The presentation of the bloody sheets. The whole take the virgin bride, wedding night. I don't think I would have been born otherwise. My father had enough respect for the Famiglia but his responsibilities toward his wife and the Famiglia ended that night. My grandfather died six years later, that's the day our father became the head of the family and moved back with me to the US. Like I said, our world functions differently and marriages aren't forged out of love, but my father only ever loved one woman."

I grab the bottle of wine and give both our glasses a refill. "What happened to your mom? You mentioned your dad taking you back to the US, did she stay in Italy?"

He gives me a sad smile. "She died giving birth to me."

I lean against him and place my head on his shoulder. "I'm so sorry."

"Did you know your mother was forced to marry the asshole who pretended to be your father? Seems our families didn't differ a lot when it came to arranged marriages."

My head whips up and I stare at him. All of this sounds insane and yet at the same time it all falls into place. The fights they had regularly, the things they used to throw at each other. And when I look into

Clemente's eyes and recognize his familiar eyes I also see when I stare in the mirror…I know he speaks the truth. Not to mention the way my mother used to react when she left to visit her friend.

"Did…does…my father. Shit. I should probably be calling him Spencer now. Did…did Spencer know I'm not his biological daughter? Was he aware about your father and my mother, about me?" I ask.

"From what my father told me, Spencer should have known since she was pregnant when my dad left. When my father couldn't stay away from your mother, he arranged to accidentally run into her and they stayed in close contact until she died."

"I remember that, you and I were there too. It was one of the rare times I saw my mother smile her radiant smile. I still can't believe she killed herself. I mean, she could have gotten a divorce, right? She wanted to, she already moved out of the house to create some distance because of all the fighting. If your father and my mother…sorry, I'm thinking in fairytales."

"When Spencer found out she was seeing my father behind his back he tried to forbid her from seeing him, even if they weren't living together anymore. There's a lot more at stake here than just people in love, ripped apart and both married, only to find each other after all those years, Gracy. There are companies involved. A status to uphold and a whole lot of money thrown into the mix and that's where things get dangerous."

"Again with the danger," I mutter and lean back to take another sip of my wine.

Clemente leans back too and the both of us watch the sunset as darkness wraps around us. There's so much more to say and talk about but there's a lot already running through my head I need to process. Besides, the wine is taking the edge off and I don't think this is a good time to be sober, though it's not a good time to get drunk either.

The mere thought of knowing who my biological father is, my mother's past, and my father...Spencer's reaction. I need more wine to let this settle and process. Come morning I will be able to wrap my head around it. Before he heads home Clemente and I decide to have dinner later this week.

I should head home too but I've had three glasses of wine and I shouldn't be driving. So, I decide to stay here instead. I shoot Eddie a text to tell him I'll drop Finn off tomorrow morning. I open another bottle of wine and decide to have one more drink before going below deck to fix something to eat.

—— CHAPTER FIVE ——

EDDIE

I'm doubting my own sanity as I get on my bike and ride over to the marina. I should be heading over to meet with Yates and a few other brothers he's reached out to. Yates and I have set things in motion to take back what's rightfully mine but we need to let others know what's about to go down. It's tricky, though. Yates isn't completely sure about a few brothers on which side they are.

Apparently, Rush has promised them loads of cash without any effort. Of course, it's dirty business he's put his sticky fingers in and that's not something we want the club connected with. But like I said, the asshole does have some bikers wanting to lean this way so we have to be careful who we approach before I walk into the clubhouse. Even more because Rush is the type of leader who forces his way and uses force against those who stand up to him.

That's also why I'm questioning my sanity. I was set to keep my distance from Gracy but seeing her hugging Clemente made utter rage flow through my veins. It doesn't make sense and maybe it's the whole "if I can't have her no one can." But right now, as I park my bike and head to her boat, I leave it all behind me. My mother told me all about her and how they met and how fucked-up her father is. A father who turned out not to be her biological father.

Man, how can Clemente just throw that little piece of information at her as if it's nothing? But, to be honest, I'm glad she's not connected to this asshole, Spencer, by blood because I've dealt with him before, he's a fucking snake. But all of this is something that slams into a person, and when I received her text, I had to go to her to make sure she's alright.

It's pitch dark on her boat and I'm not liking this

one damn bit. A woman all alone late at night, even if I know this marina must have some form of security, and she has Finn with her, she shouldn't be here all alone. Not with the information Clemente shared with her on top of everything.

I get on board and I hear Finn coming my way and the murmur of a faint, "No, no, Finn, stay here."

I scoop Finn up and walk to the front where Gracy is trying to get up. There's an empty bottle of wine and a new bottle right next to it. I put Finn down just in time to catch Gracy who stumbles over her own feet. The both of us curse for different reasons. Gracy about the pillows trying to tackle her and me for her drinking too much on a damn boat.

I bend down and take her into my arms and head below deck. I give a short whistle and Finn grabs his stuffed shark and follows me down. I have to say, this is one damn fine boat. There's a wide space with a tiny kitchen, a large couch split in two so it covers half the space left and right along with two tables in front of it. A TV is plastered against one of the cabinets across the kitchen and in the back is a door where I imagine the bedroom is.

Gracy slaps my shoulder. "Put me down, I was going to fix something to eat."

"You shouldn't have had all that wine," I grumble.

"You're not my father," she shoots back and snorts, "I already had that position doubled today. Cleared up. Switched. Clarified. Whatever. I'm hungry."

Her feet hit the floor and she heads for the kitchen. When she passes Finn she mutters, "Go, Finn! At least one of us gets to have happy hump time." She pulls open the refrigerator and bends over. "I could use some serious hump time. I need it more than food." She shoots up and glances at me. Dead serious she asks, "Any chance you want to rethink the whole no sex thing? Because I'd be willing to do the whole down and dirty thing and move on as if nothing happened."

She sidesteps as if the boat is going through rocky weather. "And I'm not just saying it because I'm drunk, because I'm not."

Right. I'm pretty sure I could get tipsy from her breath alone if I'd kiss the fuck out of her right now. I'm glad I went against my better judgement and headed over to her. And I can't believe Clemente left her alone to get drunk on a damn boat.

I stalk toward her and grab her by the shoulders to guide her to the side. I bend down to have a look into the refrigerator myself and glance around before checking some of the cabinets to see what I can whip up for us to eat.

"We're not going to have sex, Gracelynn. And it has nothing to do with you being sober, tipsy, or drunk. I need for you to be safe. And that means I can't get involved with you, no matter how badly I want you… it's not safe."

"We'd be safe if you use a condom, doofus," she says and rolls her eyes.

Yes. Definitely sober as fuck.

"I don't have a condom on me, darlin'." I can't help but chuckle and I can't think of another answer as I gather some stuff to make spaghetti.

"Aw, shucks." She sighs overdramatically and plunks down on the couch next to the kitchen. "I'm not on the pill or anything because I haven't had sex in years. Stupid guys. Did you ever notice the different types of guys and how you can tell with one glance if someone is trying to hide their personality? It's in the eyes. People who are rotten on the inside always hide things. It's a gleam. I knew my father…who in fact turned out not to be my father at all…he has the gleam. I should have known. I wish my mother would have left him sooner and had her happily ever after with my biological father. Life really sucks. Like major sucking. Like more than the best blow job I ever gave. Shit. Forget that last part. I give good blow jobs. I just meant the way I hollow my cheeks til the max, the whole ultimate sucking experience."

The pan I was holding clatters to the floor. "Could you stop fucking talking about blow jobs for one damn minute? Fuck!"

Just what I need, a visual in my head about her giving the best damn blow job while I haven't had sex in years. I could come in my goddamn pants with the mere thought of Gracy on her knees in front of me, my dick in her mouth while her supernova eyes glance up at me, silently begging me to fuck her mouth until I fire my cum down her throat.

"You're thinking about me giving you one, aren't you?" She giggles. She fucking giggles!

I should shove my dick into her mouth as payback, but instead I bend down to grab the pan and put it underneath the tap to rinse it, keeping my hands busy and trying to clear my head along with it.

"Want me to help?" Gracy quips from right beside me.

"Motherfucker," I mutter and try to calm my raging heart.

"What are we making?"

"Definitely not babies," my mind offers and I clear my throat to answer her. "Spaghetti."

"Yum. I'll help." Suddenly she doesn't seem drunk at all when she starts to roam around the kitchen.

We work side by side in the little space until she bends down right in front of me to grab a bottle of water from the refrigerator. The visual before me where I long to grab her ass is one I itch to make reality. Need I mention she's wearing a damn bikini and has some flimsy scarf wrapped around her waist?

It would be so easy to rip off the scarf, shove those bikini bottoms to the side and slide my dick home. I'm still staring when she shoves a water bottle into my hands.

"Here, drink. Looks like you need to cool down." The mischief in her eyes is tempting me to drag her close and kiss her.

Come to think of it, she doesn't look as drunk as she seemed when I got here. "How much wine did you have?"

She shrugs. "Probably a little more than half a bottle but it took me hours."

"You faked being drunk off your ass?" I state.

"Yup." She gives me devilish smile. "Nice way to test you and to give myself an advantage in case you did have bad intentions. You know, underestimate a drunk woman and all."

"Your thought process is plausible," I grumble.

A sexy giggle rings through the air and it makes our gaze connect. In this moment there's static noise filling my ears and I only have eyes for her. The way her chest rises and falls, the longing in her supernova gaze and the way her lips part.

Fuck it.

I reach for her and wrap my fingers around the nape of her neck to pull her forward as I bend down to meet in the middle as our lips crash together in a rough kiss. A slight gasp escapes her but it quickly turns into a moan. Her tiny hands slide over my chest as she grabs fistfuls of fabric to keep me close.

Her taste is addictive as my tongue slides in and starts a slow dance with hers. Electrical. As if my body is charging for what's to come. My dick hardens against her and desperately needs to be brought out of the confinement of my jeans.

My other hand slides to her ass to pull her closer and to knead it. Soft. Firm. So fucking perfect. I press her against the counter but I feel like it's not enough. Using both hands I lift her up on the counter so she can wrap her legs around me. I pull slightly back to cup her breast and boldly slide her bikini top to the side to reveal her tight nipple that's begging for my mouth.

Leaning in I let my tongue trail a path around her areola before I graze her nipple with my teeth. Her fingers roam through my hair as she pulls me closer and moans the way I want her to when I ultimately slide my dick between the lips of her pussy. Dammit, I need to be inside her. Now.

Hissing draws our attention and the both of us jump into action when the spaghetti starts to boil over. I would like nothing more than to turn off the stove and ignore the whole damn world so I can bury myself inside Gracy, but the moment is shattered and she seems to give all of her attention to finishing the spaghetti.

"You can sit down, I'll finish up," she says and I have my confirmation.

Too fast, too damn soon, but it felt so right to have her in my arms. And maybe it's for the best because we don't have a condom and she's not on the pill. Still. It's a damn shame we have to wait, but she's absolutely worth it.

I clear my throat and ask, "Where do you keep the plates?"

She gives me a shy smile and points the spoon she's holding in the direction of a cabinet. I grab two plates and place everything on the table. Gracy carries the spaghetti over to the table and starts to divide some onto the two plates.

I'm having a hard time keeping a straight face when she actually starts to eat as if she's in a restaurant, curling the spaghetti around a fork with a little help from a spoon, but all too soon she takes one string of spaghetti and closes her eyes to suck hard and lets it bounce left and right around her mouth before it disappears inside.

Instead of eating, all I can do is stare at her. Even if she's high-class and the shit she just had thrown on her lap—not to mention me kissing the fuck out of her only mere moments ago—she takes this tiny piece of time to enjoy her food carelessly. Not one hint of awkwardness but instead the woman in front of me is enjoying her food as if she's alone in the room.

Maybe it's because I've always been around other types of women because they don't hold a candle to the woman who's sitting across from me. And it's not just about the food either. The way she gives it to me straight, her beauty, her delightful character, it's the whole package. Besides, my body never reacted the way it did when my hands were on this damn fine woman.

"Aren't you hungry?" Gracy asks as she grabs a napkin and wipes her mouth clean.

Or at least she tries to, but the red sauce made her mouth slightly orange. I grab my fork and scoop some pasta into my mouth but finish it the way she's been doing and it earns me a blast of giggles that makes my dick twitch.

"How did it go with your friend Yates? Everything

okay?" she asks and picks up her fork and spoon.

"It's more complicated than I thought. It's also the reason I reached out to Clemente. Well, I was under the assumption I reached out to the person in charge, Clemente's uncle. Who we'd normally approach, and since I have been gone for a while I had no clue Clemente took over."

I don't want to drag her into my mess but she helped me out with Yates, this is the best answer I could give her with less information and yet enough to end it.

"His uncle used to be in charge but handed it over to his brother when Clemente and his father moved back to the US. Clemente took over because his father had a heart attack the day my mother died. Clemente said he hasn't been the same ever since. That's the reason my brother took over. Gosh, it's weird to say brother. I've known him for a while and we always got along great, though I haven't seen him since my mother's funeral and now all of a sudden he's…family." She puts down the spoon and fork and picks up her napkin to mindlessly twiddle with it.

I reach out and cover her hand with mine. "I know what it's like to have your world shake on its foundation. There's no rush at all to get back on your feet after you've been knocked over, you know that, right? Take your time and you'll find your strength to set things right again."

"Aren't you Mr. Positive." She snorts and then her face turns serious. "I've also told Clemente I won't stop seeing you. Not that I'm seeing you, but...well, the two of you were having this heated discussion about you pulling me into the mess you're wrapped in, and then you mentioning how Clemente is judging you and ignores the fact he's the boss of—" She falls silent and whispers to herself, "The boss of what? That sentence was never finished because Clemente cut you off. Famiglia. Arranged marriage. His father took over as head of the Famiglia. Oh. My. God. Clemente is like... like...the mob? Is he a godfather or something? This can't be happening. My ass landed into a bad movie. Okay, guys, you can come out with the cameras now. I know this insanity can't be real. Oh, shit. This can't be real, right? Tell me I'm imagining things, Eddie. I have a very vivid imagination that's gone haywire. Come on, say something."

Fuck. Why did that asshole give her information

and not mention anything about his family? "Clemente didn't tell you anything?"

"Would I be asking you this if he told me?" she hisses in anger.

"Hey, don't be angry at me," I shoot back and shove my plate away from me as I grab a napkin to wipe my mouth.

She takes her head in her hands and mutters, "We agreed to be friends, Eddie. Please, as my friend, tell me if I'm the half-sister of a mafia guy."

"Not just any mafia guy, Gracelynn." I lean back and give it to her straight. "Clemente is head of the biggest mafia family and practically runs the underworld of California."

"Well, I guess if you're going to do something, you'd better give it your all, right? Holy shit. Really? The head? The biggest? Great. Well, I already had the big name of wealth and high-class connected to my ass, I might as well add the underworld to it too, right? Shit. My life is such a mess."

"Eating spaghetti is a mess, darlin'," I chuckle and reach out to wipe the corner of her mouth with my thumb. "From what my Ma told me, you're a strong one who can handle everything."

Her eyes go down and a faint blush spreads over her cheeks. "Running the estate and cutting my father out of my life isn't really a show of strength, Eddie."

"About your father," I grumble. "And I really hate bringing it up, but I see no other way around it because not telling you feels wrong somehow."

"Well, don't you think with the big news bang of hearing I have a half-brother, and with it my father wasn't actually my father, is kinda hard to top? So, cut the whole 'hate bringing it up' and just get it out already. Wait. Is this about my father as in the bio-logical one or the non-biological one? Shit. This is so frustrating."

"I'm talking about Spencer."

"Ah, the one who married my mother for money, the fake, asshole father, gotcha," she grumbles.

"When I mentioned your name to Yates he said I couldn't trust you."

"What?" she gasps. "Are you kidding me? Not trust me? He doesn't even know me. I should have punched him in the gut harder than I already did. What an ass."

She starts to curse and I hold up my hand to stop

her. "Let me explain." She huffs and it makes her even more adorable. "It was your last name that set him off. Yates found out that Rush has been having secret meetings with Spencer for quite some time now."

Shit. I shouldn't have added that part. She doesn't need to know every detail, and yet maybe she does. "If I tell you something it needs to stay between us, understood?"

"Understood." The fierceness in her voice is something I respect.

"Rush wants to pull my MC into dealing drugs as a major money income. Drugs that need to be transported and he needs an investor, among other things, to set things in motion. A partner so to say."

"That's bad. That's very bad," she muses. Her eyes suddenly narrow as they lock on mine. "This MC of yours, are you into shady business like Rush? I've seen movies, watched TV, and read books. Bikers aren't all sweet and nice, and ride on the right side of the law. They dabble in weapons, prostitution, drugs, assassins, all that stuff that leads to a rap sheet for miles on end. Wait…why were you in prison?"

"Are you judging a man who just got out of jail?"

I can't hide the smile she brings out of me as she's sitting across from me with a determined look on her face to get to the bottom of this.

"I'm not judging, Eddie. I'm trying to make sense of it all. You know. Me, a woman who thought her life was slightly dysfunctional with my parents not getting along, while there were clearly other things going on. Then there's you, and your problems, and you suddenly mention drug deals, and Spencer having meetings because of it. Oh, and let's add Clemente into it too. You know, my mafia boss brother. Ugh. And we're back to you, walking out of prison and wanting your MC back."

"Like I said, I was set up. Rush betrayed me by forging papers about shit I didn't do. Then I thought I could trust the club's attorney but she was fucking Rush so they were working together. By the time I figured it all out I was in jail. And no, we don't do any shady business like drugs or guns. I have several businesses and one of those is being a silent partner in a construction company that used to be my father's but now belongs to my mother. It's where most of my brothers work. So, you can say this MC works in construction. And before you comment with things that pop up in your head…no, we've never hidden a body in a foundation or covered one up with cement or plastered one behind a wall."

"You know that's kinda disappointing when you put it like that. No excitement at all? You guys don't do the whole gangs, trade guns, shootouts for turf thing? You make it sound less action movie and more like a boring documentary. Not that documentaries are boring. I like them. And I'm glad you keep those guys on a straight path. Though I have to say, the whole construction thing does offer opportunities for hiding a body…are you sure you guys never used the company to hide your enemies?"

A chuckle escapes me and I shake my head at the way she's clearly teasing me with her tone of voice and the twinkle in her eyes.

"That wasn't my father's intention when he started the construction company. He did it to create a job opportunity for himself and a few guys he grew up with. He built a solid friendship with five others, that's when they founded Unruly Defenders. For a place they could enjoy when they were done with work and with riding their bikes. To take a break from the workload and so on. It grew into something more, a brotherhood, a family. And I hate how Rush put an end to it. He not only stole my freedom but he ripped everything apart that my father built. My father's death might have been classified as an accident, but I have my reasons to assume Rush is responsible for the death of my father. I'm fairly sure, but I can't prove anything. And as if it wasn't enough, he also killed his dream by taking Unruly Defenders MC from me and ripping it apart by being a dictator who only cares about himself." My voice cracks due to all the emotion flowing through my veins.

Gracy slides around the table to sit next to me and leans her head on my shoulder. "You're already making a change to turn it all around, Eddie. These things take time and if what you mentioned is true, then Rush has been planning everything for a long time and you have to be careful. You've only been out for a handful of days, and you're just one man. Don't carry the weight of all of this on your own shoulders. You have to trust others like how Rush is also reaching out to Spencer. Hey, was that why you had a meeting with

Clemente?"

Fuck it. I've shared too much anyway, and talking with her takes away some of my stress and helps me get things in order inside my head. "No, like I said, I thought I was meeting with his uncle, he was the one in charge when I went away years back. We have worked together in the past when my father was still alive. Clemente's family practically run the underworld of California and have knowledge and contacts. I wanted information about Rush. Clemente warned me about him because Rush is making too many waves. He's drawing attention from both the law and the underworld."

"That's why Clemente doesn't want me near you," she muses.

"Clemente wants you safe, and so do I." I wrap my arm around her and pull her close. "But I'm afraid the both of us may want the impossible because you're tied to all of it. Clemente, Spencer..." I place a swift kiss on the top of her head. "And to me."

Admitting that last part out loud is a necessity. With everything we talked about—throwing it out in the open—I'm not about to cut the one thing out of my life that feels right. The reminder of my cellmate,

Chance, vivid in my thoughts how he spared the woman he cared about but ended up hurting the both of them in the end.

They did manage to end up together after a long road to get there, but those years were hell for the both of them. And this also is a reminder. If it's meant to be, it's meant to be. So why the hell should I fight it, or punish myself even more? I've done my sentence, it's time to move forward and take what's mine.

CHAPTER SIX

GRACY

I wake slowly and instantly realize the pillow my head is resting on is in fact not so much a pillow but Eddie's chest. Pushing myself up, I glance down and a slow smile spreads across my face as the memories of last night resurface.

After dinner we talked some more and eventually took Finn for a walk and we ended up watching a movie in bed. The both of us are still dressed and I guess somewhere during the movie we fell asleep.

I reach for Finn who's sleeping near our feet and take him in my arms as I slide off the bed. Finn knows the routine. I need to find my shoes and coat before we head out for a walk. I grab my purse and decide to swing by the tiny place near the marina to get some coffee and breakfast to take back to the boat.

Eddie is still sleeping when we get back, but as I place the coffee on the table and the bag with fresh pastries, his phone suddenly starts to ring, waking him up. He groans and grabs his phone.

With a groggy voice he says, "Yeah?"

Clearly, the person on the other end said something important because he flashes up and his eyes are wide open. "When?" Eddie scoots off the bed and rubs a hand over his face. "Then we're going to speed things up. Two hours from now I'm walking into the clubhouse. Yes. Make sure everything is set. Good. See you there, brother."

Eddie stands and puts his phone away to free up his hands so he can rub his face. Finn dashes off to him and starts to claw with his one front paw at Eddie's pants. He reaches down and scoops him up, earning him a facewash from Finn. The way that rugged man cradles his little dog in his arms makes me swoon.

He bends down and places Finn back on the floor,

who happily trots to his blanket to catch up on some sleep. "Something smells good. Did you go out for coffee?"

"Uh huh, and fresh pastries. Did something go wrong? The phone call, did Yates have news?" I question as I grab plates and place the pastries on them.

Eddie grabs a cinnamon bun and places a kiss on my temple. "Don't worry about it," he mutters and takes a bite.

"I am, and I will. And after last night I kinda hoped you would be honest with me. And I know there are things you can't tell me and aren't my business, but you can't expect me not to care about you." I quickly grab my coffee and take a sip to stop myself from rambling.

Eddie's gaze is locked on me as he slowly eats his cinnamon bun.

He reaches for his coffee and says, "Yates called to say Rush wants everyone in church this afternoon. There will be a vote. I need to prevent it from happening."

"He's going to push this whole dealing in drugs thing through, isn't he?" My heartbeat picks up. Not due to fear, but from anger. "You need to stop him. You mentioned last night how all eyes are on Unruly Defenders because of him. Dammit, what if he is doing this because he wants you to walk in there and claim your spot as the president? And then have the cops come in and you'll be the one with the criminal record and right back where you were a few days ago."

Eddie stares at me with wide eyes and it makes me feel weird.

"I'm overthinking things, right? Too farfetched? Sorry. My mind is running in different directions and I just want you safe and out of trouble."

"Not farfetched at all," Eddie muses. "Why didn't I think about this particular angle? Shit. Can I trust Yates? Is he in on all this?"

"Wait. Hang on, and put a pin in it, Mister. Are you questioning your buddy's loyalty again? That's not my intention, Eddie. And really, you can't flip a coin with trust and not trust a person. I get you've been betrayed, and Rush is a scumbag and all, but there are more loyal people out there than scumbags. And you'd better stay on the positive side of things. Your mother tells me you practically are Mister Positive, always have been.

Hell, I've even called you that myself. So, don't let that scumbag crush another part of you. Am I clear?"

"You're damn sexy when you get all angry and tell me what I can and can't do," he tells me with a wolfish grin on his face.

"Yeah, well, you're damn sexy every damn minute of the day," I mutter and stuff my mouth full with a large bite of a cinnamon bun.

We finish our coffee and I gather my things before the both of us leave the boat. Finn and I follow Eddie to his bike where it's parked near my car. I put Finn in the car so I can give Eddie my full attention.

He delicately strokes his fingertips along my hair and cups the back of my neck to pull me close. "If only we met a few years ago," he whispers, more to himself than to me.

"Time is irrelevant. And problems will always come and go. A life can be lost by tripping in your own home or taking one step outside. Does this mean you're not supposed to live? That you should be too scared to take a risk and avoid doing things that feel good, or make you curious, or make you crave so badly your heart aches to connect with that single person?

Except, you don't want to take that step because the future is unsure, the consequences could take lives... and yet, by not doing it and playing it safe, you did in fact already kill everything beforehand. Your own life, your future, everything. Because you're not living it. And I'm rambling. But it's frustrating. You are frustrating." My shoulders sag. "I know this whole situation is not on you or on me. I didn't choose the insanity my life is wrapped in, and you didn't choose to be betrayed. It happened to you, it happened to the both of us. Just…don't let it define you."

I reach out and stand on my toes to connect my lips to his. I pull back and stare in his eyes to see the turmoil swirling in there. I pat his chest and turn to head for my car. Getting inside, I start the engine, making the radio automatically turn on. The tunes of Danny Vera's song "Roller Coaster" fill the car.

I love his tunes but this song and the timing is practically melodically shoving my nose into the fact of the turmoil of life. It takes everything inside me not to stop the car and rush back into his muscled arms. But instead I take one last glance at him through the rearview mirror as I head home.

My whole mood is down the drain when I park my car and head for the bungalow I share with Maggie. I've never had a guy influence my feelings how Eddie seems to be able to rock them. Good or bad. And I hate it even more that I don't have a grip on myself.

And why do I even care? I just met him a few days ago. Hell, we've only spent time together for a handful of hours spread out over two days. And I didn't even see him for three days after the first time we met. Not to mention he was an ass that first day. Great, Gracy, just great. Now I'm fussing over wanting him while I have so many other things running havoc in my life.

I stalk inside and Finn rushes to Maggie who is waiting for me. Suddenly I feel bad about not letting her know where I was last night. It's not like I owe her an explanation but I know how she worries about me. And to be honest, I never spent a night somewhere else without telling her.

"Sorry. I went out to the boat but didn't intend to spend the night there." I place my purse on the table and decide to grab a quick shower before I head for work.

I'm about to head for my room but Maggie's voice

stops me. "Eddie called last night to let me know where you two were. And you don't owe me an apology, sweetheart. You know that. Oh, and I will take over your shift this morning because I need for you to run a few errands for me."

"Sure, just let me grab a shower and a change of clothes and I'll take care of it for you." It's not unusual for Maggie to rearrange my day but my gut tells me there's more to it this time. "What do you need me to do?"

"You go and get ready, I'll make you a list." She shoos me away and even if I think it's weird, there's a hot shower with my name on it screaming for me to take it.

I head for my room and decide to take my time freshening up. Standing before my closet, it's easy to make a choice what to wear. Mainly because I don't have to be behind a desk today. Ripped blue jeans, a purple tank top, along with some black boots with a tiny heel. Most definitely a day for casual clothes.

I grab some underwear and my thoughts slide to Eddie again. Why can't I ban him from my mind? Sliding the purple lace panties on—along with the matching bra—I dress quickly and decide to leave my hair down. I glance at my makeup and I don't want to fuss too much and only apply some mascara along with some lip gloss.

Ready to take on a new day and dead set not to think about Eddie, I stroll into the living room to find Maggie, but she's not here. The sliding doors are open and I know she likes to drink her tea on the patio, so I head out and see her sitting in her favorite chair while glancing at the beach.

"I'm ready, do you have your list of errands for me?" I question and her eyes land on me.

"Eddie has the list, he's outside waiting for you," she simply says and I swear I can feel my eyes widen and my jaw drop.

I start to sputter but she just shakes her head while wearing a smile, freaking mischief dancing in her eyes. "Just hear him out, sweetheart. Remember what I told you."

"I remember what you told me, but I feel like a freaking marionette. Everyone is trying to pull my strings their way and I have no other choice but to ride the waves others create while I can't seem to get my own life on track. And I am trying with Eddie but the whole being betrayed thing? That's not a knife in the back leaving a scar, it's one huge gaping wound that asshole Rush is rubbing salt in and it's still wide open, unable to heal. He doesn't trust anyone, and even the slightest turn makes him doubt stuff." The words leave my mouth and they ring hard in my own ears and it makes me come to a conclusion. "You're right. He needs me. He needs a friend, and I like him."

Maggie stands and closes the distance between us. She places her hands on my shoulders and softly says, "He does need you. I know he might be difficult to be around at times, believe me, I married his father, remember? But he's loyal and honest. You need him as much as he needs you." Her hands tighten on my shoulders and she pulls me into a hug. "You're young and free, sweetheart. Do what feels right."

My throat closes up, and in this moment, I miss my mother even more but I'm thankful to have Maggie in my life. Her kind words and loving arms are just the thing I need to see through the obstacles in my life. Even if she's biased with Eddie being her son, she's also there for me.

She pulls back and gives me a smile and it makes me mutter, "It's a good thing my mascara is water-proof."

The both of us snicker and Maggie gives me a little push. "Go on, he's waiting outside."

I tell her goodbye and give Finn a quick hug before I grab my purse and head out. Eddie is on his phone and is right next to Yates. The both of them are sitting on their bikes. My heart skips a beat by the way Eddie looks, wearing a leather cut with patches on it.

Eyeing one of the patches as I walk closer, I can tell there are two skulls merged into one, a human one and a bull one. A rose sits slightly behind the skulls on each side, and everything is held together by two daggers.

"I almost didn't recognize you there," Eddie quips right after he ends the call. "All dressed up as my old lady."

Yates chuckles and slaps him on the back. "Nice touch, man. Very smooth way to claim your woman."

Old lady? Claim your woman? I'm about to question him but my phone starts to ring inside my purse. Digging deep, I grab hold and see it's Clemente calling.

"Hey, Clemente. I'm in the middle of something, can I call you back?" I ask.

Clemente didn't even seem to have heard one word I told him. His voice barks in anger, "Is it true? You're his old lady? I thought I told you yesterday to be careful and not get involved with him, Gracy."

There's that term again, old lady.

"Clemente," I sigh. "I have no clue what you're talking about. And I absolutely don't appreciate receiving a call from you where you're throwing words at me in anger, so either explain in a normal way or I'm hanging up."

Eddie is standing in front of me and leans in to whisper words on a hot breath right next to my ear, making goose bumps erupt to run wild across my skin. "You were right, darlin'. And I'm taking that step, even if the future is unsure. The whole craving part was what hit me. And since I'm taking back what belongs to me, I'm also taking what should belong to me. You. My old lady."

"Did you hear a word I just said?" Clemente says, suddenly sounding very tired.

"Sorry. Someone was distracting me. But to answer your question…yes, I'm Eddie's old lady."

Whatever that might entail because I'm not completely sure what comes with this title. I've seen movies, series, read books, and the old lady term did swing by as the name they give the girlfriend, wife, married biker style, whatever. Besides, when you get thrown into stormy waters and someone throws you a lifeline that makes you feel safe and gives you something solid to hold onto…you grab hold and rail that sucker in. And that's exactly what I'm doing.

"Walk away, Gracy. I'm sending a car over and you're moving in with me or I'll get you an apartment. I want you out of there. Now," Clemente growls.

My eyes widen slightly and I see Eddie reach for my phone. Still standing close to me, I'm positive he heard what Clemente just said. But I'm the one he threw those words at and I'm beyond pissed.

"Look, Clemente. Yesterday was the first time I saw you in almost nine months. You seemed to have known for a while now that I am your half-sister. I just found out. I'm not holding a grudge because you didn't tell me the second you knew. Well, maybe, but my point is…don't act like you're my big brother and I suddenly need to be protected. And I most certainly won't move into your house or live in an apartment you supply. I have a fat bank account myself and don't need anything from anyone."

"You don't understand," Clemente says, his tone now filled with concern.

"No, Clemente, you don't understand." I take a deep breath and tell him, "Family is supposed to have your back no matter what decision you make. You of all people should understand the value of making your own decision, with the restrictions and obligations of the Famiglia. And even if you think a person is making a mistake, it's still theirs to make and find out for themselves they've fucked-up."

"Okay, Gracy," Clemente groans. "I have a feeling there's little I can refuse you, so I'll have your back. But remember I'm your family now and I'm here no matter what. Tell Eddie I'll get it done. And you call me when you need me."

We exchange our goodbyes and I end the call but keep staring at my phone. I've always liked Clemente and as he mentioned with the not being able to refuse me anything…he always did say he had a soft spot when it came to me. But I thought it was because his father was a good friend of my mother. I release an unfeminine snort at the thought of the head of a mafia family having a soft spot for me.

"Everything okay?" Eddie murmurs and places his finger underneath my chin to make sure I connect my gaze with his.

"Everything is overwhelming and now you add this whole old lady thing to it too. What does it all entail? This old lady thing? Are we a thing? And why am I mentioning to you that Clemente said he'll get it done?"

"It's something between me and Clemente, nothing you have to be worried about. And you being my old lady means I claimed you, you're mine. You could say we're a thing but being my old lady has a lot more weight to it than two people being a thing. I'll explain later, for now we need to go. I'm heading to the clubhouse and I need for you to come with me, okay?"

"Why do I feel like you're not giving me a choice? Are you getting bossy already? Is that how things are going to be between us?" I grumble, wondering what exactly I signed myself up for by agreeing to be his old lady.

"Darlin'," he drawls in a husky tone. "You haven't seen me bossy yet. And I'll show you later today exactly how things are going to be between us. When we're alone, and naked."

I can feel my whole face heat up. Did he really just imply having sex and voice it hard enough for Yates to hear?

I clear my throat and decide to ignore his last statement. "Let's go, did you want me to drive behind you guys?"

"No, your ass needs to be on the back of my bike," Eddie says and guides me to his bike.

Good thing I opted for jeans and boots instead of a summer dress. He grabs a helmet and puts it on my head himself. Yates watches the both of us closely. I should question why Eddie suddenly decided to be with me while this morning he thought he couldn't because of everything that was going on. Maybe it is as simple as him taking my advice about what I said to him this morning.

Except the words Clemente made me mention

to Eddie strike me as odd and it makes me feel as if there's more going on than I'm aware of. But for now, I wrap my arms around Eddie's waist and relish in the way I feel when I hug him close as the bike roars to life underneath us.

—— CHAPTER SEVEN ——

EDDIE

She feels so fucking good and I feel so damn bad for doing this. I should be completely honest and yet, deep down I am, but I really would have wanted to do this differently. Namely without the implying ulterior motives that can make it seem I made this move for a whole different reason. Still, in the end, the result is the same but the reasons and the way it all went down is leaving a bad taste in my mouth.

Luckily, she only knows what's important; the fact she's mine. My old lady and I intend to keep her safe and do exactly what she said I should do. My life, my future, and I'm damn well going to live like I own it all.

My phone rings and I fish it out of my jeans. I see it's Chance calling and even if I'm seconds away from handling something that can't wait, I decide to take his call. "Chance, I'm about to head into a meeting, can I call you back in an hour or so?"

"You could, or we could have a drink later today if the offer still stands and you have room for us," Chance says.

I glance down at Gracy, because if anyone knows if there's room at the estate, it's her. "Hang on, Chance, let me check." I hold the phone slightly away from my mouth and ask, "Do you know if we have a bungalow available for the weekend?"

Her eyebrows scrunch up for a moment before she nods. "Yes, I think there are two available. Shall I call Travis and have him book one? What name?"

I give her a smile and handle the phone call first. "Chance, everything is set. Feel free to bring Pixy along with you. What time will you be at the estate? Good. I'll swing by later tonight."

I disconnect the line and tell Gracy, "Chance

Bateman and his girl, Aubrey Bloom. Can you give Travis a heads-up?"

Gracy grabs her phone and within a few seconds everything is set and it leaves me to focus on what's in front of me. I'm both nervous and thrilled to be walking into the clubhouse.

Yates and I have been planning this and when Gracy mentioned the possibility of Rush trying to set me up again, I made sure to have something up my sleeve. That little something was just confirmed by Gracy when she mentioned Clemente was going to pull through for me.

"Are you ready, Prez?" Yates quips as he smacks my back.

I slide my arm around Gracy's waist and tuck her against me. I take a deep breath and gain strength from the woman who sneaks her arm around me to slide her fingers casually into the back pocket of my jeans as if we've been together for years.

Hardening my tone, I tell Yates, "You know as well as I that I was born to lead this MC."

"So very fucking true, brother," Yates replies, his voice laced with respect.

Yates opens the door and steps through to hold it open for us. There are a lot of bikers in the main room of the clubhouse and they're making a lot of noise until all eyes land on us. Well, mainly on me because clearly none of them were expecting me to step inside this clubhouse.

Girly sounds of excitement unleash from my right. This club always had women visit for a good time, making it easy for the brothers to have some entertainment when they're in the mood. I need to end it before it starts, but obviously I'm too late when Nikki, Rush's sister, tries to wrap her arms around my neck and with it pushes Gracy away from me. Motherfucker.

I rip her arms away from me and give a hard shove. She stumbles back and lands on her ass. A hint of satisfaction slides through me when I see her shocked face but it quickly turns to disgust. I might have let her distract me a time or two but never again. Not to mention she's Rush's sister and I know for a fact she helped him to set me up.

"Don't fucking disrespect me," I spit my words at her and reach for Gracy, who is observing all of it in silence. I'm thankful she lets me pull her against me.

"I would say it's good to be back but I guess all of you need to work at giving me a warm welcome, eh?"

Snickers flow through the room as Nikki pushes herself up and stalks through the room to stand next to her brother. Rush is spitting fire at me. The fucker obviously wasn't expecting me to walk in here. I shoot him a vicious grin and let my eyes trail to the clock on the wall. Just a few more minutes if all goes well…in other words; if Clemente pulls through like he said he would.

"I've heard you're not doing a good job leading my MC, asshole. Good thing I'm out early to take back my place and push you and every rotten seed out of my MC, before you drag this club down with you." There are only a handful of bikers swinging their gaze from me to Rush after I spilled this little detail.

Yates told over half our brothers what was going down today. Well, only the fact I was returning and he only told those he trusted and knew they were against Rush, and sick of his dictatorship. That left only a handful of bikers in the middle and those are now confused.

The three guys standing next to Rush who are also

spitting fire at me? I don't recognize any of those guys, but Yates told me about them. They are on Rush's side; he considers them his trusted men.

"A lot of things changed while you were on the inside, brother," Rush rumbles. "Times have changed and I've led this club into a profitable direction. I'd say you need to earn the right to come back, to see if you still have what it takes."

"Have what it fucking takes?" I snap, anger flowing freely through my veins. "My father founded this club. I've walked in his footsteps and I damn well bled for this club and helped it succeed. Hell, the building your filthy ass is standing in is in my fucking name, I practically am Unruly Defenders MC." I snicker and shake my head. "Have what it takes. Motherfucker. How do you even find the nerve to question my abilities while it was you who jammed a knife in my back and left me to rot in a jail cell so you could steal what belonged to me and my family? And look what you fucking did with it. Dragging the club's name into the dirt and tainting it with your need for drugs and money, only to want more and more. Unless you wanted all of us to rot in a fucking jail cell, then you're doing a damn fine job with the heat you're bringing upon everyone in here. Because that's the only place your leadership takes you and everyone else."

Rush stomps forward at the same time sirens faintly start to blare. I shove Gracy behind me because I knew this confrontation was coming. Yates has my back. We talked this through since I needed to make sure no harm would come to her.

I don't think twice and in two steps I'm close enough to whip my arm back and take a swing at Rush. A right hook connects with his jaw and right after I jab my other fist underneath his chin. He stumbles back and shakes his head in an effort to clear it enough to fight back.

Useless, because the entire time I was in prison all I did was make sure I kept pushing my body into shape. Easy enough to do when your focus is on getting out and having your revenge. But I've always been training and fighting, even before I ended up behind steel bars. This club has a ring on the back of the property where we have fights every Saturday night for entertainment and to blow off some steam when needed.

A harmless bet between brothers or to fight out

your differences. The ring is used for a lot of reasons and it also keeps us on our toes and in shape. But it seems Rush didn't keep the tradition going because his effort to swing his fist in the direction of my head is useless. It gives me the opportunity to jab him in the gut, making him double over.

The sirens are becoming louder and it's clear they're coming from right outside the clubhouse. Satisfaction flows freely through me and I can't help the big grin sliding over my face. Payback, motherfucker.

My father and I have worked with Clemente's uncle a lot of times in the past. When you need something done or have issues or anything, you don't go to the authorities, you go to the head of the family that runs the underworld. They have all the connections—and the information—along with the possibilities to get shit done.

In the previous meeting I had with Clemente, I asked him to get me all the information and background about Rush. But I was surprised to hear Rush already had drawn the unwanted attention of the underworld as well as the law.

This was also the reason Clemente advised me not

to interfere, because the DEA recently linked Rush with a shipment of drugs and was waiting for him to meet with the dealer and the one who financed it, so they could roll up the complete network.

Now, I'm not one to be patient, and with Rush dragging the club down with it, I felt I had no other choice but to interfere. Gracy being Clemente's half-sister and the way he stood up for her in my presence made me aware he would do anything for her. I know damn well how unfair it is to twist faith a bit to speed things up.

In my talk with Yates he suggested we use Gracy's connection and make Clemente help us so he could get the DEA to act now and arrest Rush. Needless to say, with the screaming sirens, our plan worked. Though, it leaves a bad taste in my mouth to use Gracy this way.

Me and her would have happened along the way anyhow because the talk she gave me this morning made me see things clearly. I should take everything I want, and damn well live my life to the fullest or I wouldn't be alive at all. That's why I set things in motion with getting my club and my girl.

But the bottom line stays the same, I fought dirty

but I needed to get things done and to keep Gracy safe along with it. I can justify it in every direction but if someone should hint or say something… Gracy would think I used her to get what I want and it won't matter that my feelings for her are legit. Even if I just met her, she's the one woman who ignites feelings inside me I never knew I had or wanted. Let's just hope everything goes smooth and we can move forward.

"They're comin' for you, asshole," Rush grunts. "What did you do? Break out of jail? Was it worth it? Because you're going back and I'm here to fucking stay and do with this club as I please. This club is mine. My father assured me everything would be mine one day but he never had the guts to stand up and take it. I have. I'm the new generation setting a new course."

"You're insane, Rush. Your father was my father's VP, his friend, a founding member. This club was built for brotherhood. Family. Loyalty. Your father like mine had great plans in mind and the both of them had their eye set on the future. None of it involved drugs or a dictatorship. You're the one fucking up, wanting the money in your hand and the coke up your nose. Everything you do taints your already twisted brain.

Our fathers are turning in their graves knowing the shit you did."

"You've always had your head in the sand, Eddie. My father was using the club to make quick cash exactly the way I've been doing. When he died, I took over that side of the family business so to say. And with the whole two birds, one stone…getting your father finally out of the way along with it, I had the chance to step up and expand. That's what I've been doing, expanding business. Evolve. It's how shit's done, but my father didn't understand either. Now, get out of my fucking clubhouse and crawl back to your jail cell where you belong. And don't think the little cunt beside you will be any help. I know she's the daughter of Spencer Lightners but let me tell you…that fucker is in bed with me. I'm the one with the right connections. Seeing the cunt's time is ticking away as we speak, dear old Spencer will finally have it all, and she won't be an issue anymore either. With Spencer being my partner in crime so to say, that right there gives me privilege over you. I guess that gives me all the right to be the one boning his daughter, don't you think? Better hand her over too then, pretty boy."

I see red and launch myself forward to kill this asshole with my bare hands but I'm being held back by Yates.

This doesn't stop Rush from spilling some more words when he leans in and says, "Look at you, isn't that the story of your life? Being held back by everything while others take what's there for the taking. Be fucking glad I put you in a jail cell because my own damn sister wanted you to live because she has this stupid crush on you. I gave in because Nikki played out her part and I need her from time to time, but if it was up to me, I'd give you the same treatment I gave your father and mine."

"Motherfucker," I roar and fight my VP because Rush just openly admitted to killing my father as well as his own.

"Get a hold of yourself, Eddie," Yates growls in my ear. "The cops just came inside. If you attack him you're going to jail too. Calm. Down."

Gracy plasters herself against me and I instantly wrap my arms around her.

"Better come here, sugar. Daddy will be more pleased if you'd ride my cock instead of this jailbait,"

Rush rumbles.

Yates' back is in front of me as he's facing Rush and jabs his chest before I can so much as blink. "You're the one with your head in the sand, asshole. Because Spencer Lightners isn't connected with this woman by blood. But you know who is? Clemente Dimentello. Now that name rings a fucking bell so loud your ears bleed, don't you think? Yeah, who's fucked now, huh? You asshole, because Eddie here is the only one with the right connections thanks to the old lady he just claimed."

Fuck. Why the hell did Yates have to say that last part? I feel Gracy tense up in my arms and when I glance down and stare into her eyes, they are filled with hurt and confusion. I know everything is about to shatter and I can't do shit to stop it because the DEA is bursting through the door and starting to yell out demands.

It takes over an hour for the clubhouse to get back to normal when the DEA finally leaves. Rush is gone and I need to get back into the main clubhouse because all of us were taken apart one by one to get checked over and have our personal information taken and for sure they took their time checking me. When I stalk back into the main room, I glance over every head but don't see Gracy.

Rhett steps closer and asks, "What do you need, Pres?"

"My old lady, did you see where she went?"

Rhett shakes his head and leans over the bar. "Hudson, did you see if Pres' old lady left or know where she might be?"

Hudson stalks over to me. "I didn't pay attention. Maybe she's in the bathroom, you know how chicks are."

I hear laughter and see it's Maxton lifting his beer at me. "She left you. Walked right out the door after the DEA left. Bet the bitch served her purpose and is done with your sorry ass."

"Out," I growl. "Leave your cut and get the fuck out of here."

Hudson rounds the bar and is standing in front of Maxton before I can say another word. Rhett is beside him and starts to pull at Maxton's cut.

"You don't deserve to wear this," Rhett sneers. "Finally, I don't have to look at your ugly face anymore or hear your stupid shit."

Maxton rips away from Rhett's grip and shrugs out of his cut, throwing it on the floor before Hudson's feet.

"You're all dead. Mark my fucking words. Rush will be out later today and we'll end you fuckers once and for all," Maxton spits and stomps out of the clubhouse.

Hudson glances over his shoulder at me. "I'm going to make sure that asshole leaves and then I'm going to reset the code for the gate. Anyone else we need to kick out? Den or Banjo? Those two fuckers are always...wait. Where did they go?"

"I saw them both leave right after the DEA left," Rhett quips. "Good riddance. Those four were always setting the rules and took away any options for taking stuff to the table."

Yates comes to stand next to me. "Like you mentioned, Hudson, reset the security code and make sure only the four of us know the code. The two of you can take turns keeping an eye on who goes in and out. Needless to say, none of those four fuckers are allowed back in."

"You got it, VP," Hudson states and rushes out the door.

"Rhett, get a prospect to manage the bar, and another one to round everyone up. I need every member in church within the next ten minutes. Time for a meeting so I can get all of you up to speed about things," I grunt and Rhett jumps into action. I give my attention to Yates. "I need to know where Gracy is. And fuck, man…you shouldn't have said that part about me having the right connections by claiming Gracy. You basically said I claimed her because of it."

"Shit," Yates grunts and slides his fingers through his hair. "I didn't think. I just wanted that asshole to know he didn't stand a chance against you. She has to be around here somewhere, right?"

"Maxton said Gracy walked out the door right after the DEA left. And so did Den and Banjo. Maxton just walked out that damn door too. What if they take her, or fuck…what if they already took her? Dammit." I grab my phone and dial her number.

It rings four times before she picks up.

"I don't want to talk to you," she snaps.

"Where are you?" I growl in return.

"Home. Don't bother coming over. You're a real grade A asshole, Eddie. I don't ever—"

The line goes dead and I pull the phone away from my ear to call her again but instead I see my phone's dead. Dammit, what fucking timing. I don't even have her damn number because it's only saved in my phone.

"Fuck," I roar in frustration. Though, at least I know she arrived home safely, even if she's pissed at me.

— CHAPTER EIGHT —

GRACY

I can't believe the asshole hung up on me. "Mothertrucker," I grumble as I step into the lobby, making Travis' head swing up.

"Well, good afternoon to you too." Travis closes the book he was glancing through and strolls around the desk to stand in front of it. "Do I even dare ask why you're growling?"

"Eddie," I sigh in frustration.

"Ah, sculpted abs hottie. What did he do? Flash you the goods without letting you touch it?" Travis chuckles but it stops when he sees me narrow my eyes.

"Oh, he flashed, and I touched alright. Hell, they were even mine for a mere hour or two before I realized he just used me to flash my name and statement at others," I seethe and realize I'm losing a grip on myself.

I take a steady breath and try to calm down.

"I'm sure it was all a mix up or something. Maggie's son would never be disrespectful," Travis says and I guess I'm out of my depths here.

"I only know what I heard and saw when I was pulled into his mess, Travis. But I swear it all made sense. You know what? I'm going to pack a bag and take a few days off. I'm going to talk to Maggie and tell her that I'm going to need a few days off starting now, okay?"

"Okay, sweetie. You take care of you and if there's anything I can help with or if you want to talk or just sit and drink wine, call me, okay?"

I nod absently and stomp to Maggie's bungalow. I heard the words Yates threw at Rush. I know what Eddie said to me, and how I felt, and how we connected so well together last night. And then we were together, and dammit, why is everything so freaking complicated?

Rush is an asshole taunting Eddie, and I can't imagine going through all of the stuff Eddie is dealing with. Not to mention I heard Rush insinuate he killed Eddie's father. And then the things he said about my father. No, Spencer isn't even my father.

I haven't seen Spencer in nine months. Time is ticking. Spencer will have it all. It's almost been nine months since my mother's death. Shit. My mother's will. When I left right after her funeral, we had an appointment set to go through my mother's will. What if it has to do with the inheritance? Great, now I have more to add to the long list of things going on in my life.

Then add Eddie's crazy mess to it and it's a full-blown roller coaster ride of insanity. One thing at a time. I need to clear my head and that's exactly what I'm going to do; a few days of vacation time on my boat.

But I have to talk to Maggie about it first. I'm sure she'll be fine with me taking a few days off, though. I use the key to open the door and my gut instantly knows something is wrong. I rush inside and glance around. I don't see anyone but I hear faint barking coming from the patio.

Running outside, I notice Finn is jumping his front paw on Maggie's shoulder who is lying on the ground. It seems as if she fell or, dammit. I grab my phone and call the emergency number while I drop down next to her.

Frantically I search for her pulse and at first I can't find it, but when I check again I can feel a very faint heartbeat. When I'm sure help is on the way, I know I have to call Eddie. It doesn't matter if I'm angry at him, he needs to be here.

I tap my phone and wait for him to pick up but the call goes straight to voicemail. Shit. With the way our call ended, maybe his phone died, or maybe he's ignoring me. Either way he still needs to know about Maggie. The sirens draw my attention away from my phone and I stash it back into my jeans. When I'm sure Maggie has the help she needs, I will think of a way to reach Eddie.

Luckily the ambulance gets here quick, though Maggie still hasn't regained consciousness and I'm worried if she's going to make it. I make sure to ask what hospital they are taking her to so I can follow in my car.

But first I need to have someone take care of Finn for me because I don't know how long this is going to take. I head for the lobby to ask Travis, though I know how allergic he is, but what other choice do I have? When I step inside, I see there is a couple checking in for a stay. All of their heads swing my way.

"Sorry to interrupt, but Travis...I know you're allergic, but Maggie was just taken to the hospital. She was unconscious when I found her at the bungalow. I need to get to the hospital, except Finn needs someone to look after him. And I can't reach Eddie to tell him about his mother. Please, Travis, can you?"

"Eddie's mum? Eddie Barhamer's mum?" the man checking in asks, an accent tainting his words and if I have to guess, it sounds Australian.

"Yes," I tell him but swing my head toward Travis. "I need to go now."

The man and the woman share a look and the man grabs his phone from his pocket as the woman holds her hands out to take Finn.

"We know Eddie. Well, Chance knows him better

than I do because I've only met him once." She gives me a sweet smile. "I'm Aubrey, by the way."

"Chance and Aubrey. You called Eddie earlier about a reservation. I made the reservation," I muse while automatically handing Finn over to Aubrey.

"Eddie's phone goes straight to voicemail," Chance says. "You do what you have to do. I'll keep trying to reach Eddie and we'll be here watching over Finn. You mentioned Travis here being allergic, come find us at our bungalow when everything is taken care of."

I nod warily and get ready to leave but suddenly realize Finn needs his distraction. "Wait," I gasp. "Finn needs his goat to hump."

Chance and Aubrey's eyes widen and they share a look again. "A goat?" they ask in sync.

"The three-legged dog here needs to pound away his energy so Gracy here gives him stuffed animals to blow off steam. Here," Travis says and hands over the stuffed animal, furiously sneezing three times in a row right after.

"I need to go," I croak.

"Wait, take this." Chance hands me a note with a phone number written on it. "That's my number in case you need it."

I take the note and nod before I rush out and jump in my car. My mind is still pushing me to notify Eddie and with Chance calling him just now and also going straight to voicemail along with the fact our call ended the way it did the last time I talked to him, I'm now sure his phone died.

He needs to know about his mother. If it were me, I would want someone to get me. I decide to head for the clubhouse since it's down the road anyway but when I get to the gate it's all locked and it takes a while before a voice comes through the intercom.

"I need to speak with Eddie, it's urgent," I tell the guy over the intercom.

"Look, Lady, our Prez just came back, he has other things to do instead of getting his dick wet."

If my skull could blow off from all the pumped-up steam due to my anger, it would be shooting through the roof of the car by now. Remembering the way Eddie talked to the woman launching herself at him the second he stepped foot inside the clubhouse, I gather there's one way to deal with this.

I lean in close to the intercom and snap, "Open

your fucking ears you little biker prick. You're talking to the president's old lady and you just disrespected me. Get my damn man here right now or I will drive through this fucking gate to come get you so I can rip your damn balls off, understood?"

Eddie is already rushing to me when I haven't even finished my rant and the gate is also opening. I guess the mentioning of me being his old lady was enough. I do feel better letting out the anger, though. And yet the look of relief on Eddie's face makes sadness burst through me because he thinks I came back to him while I'm only here to get him to the hospital because of his mother.

I decide to jump into action rather than dump the load of information on him. "I need for you to get in the car, Eddie," I tell him.

Yates jogs up from behind him. "Can it wait? We're in a meeting."

I give the rude idiot a glare. "No, it can't wait." I direct my attention at Eddie, knowing I have no other choice but to do it here. "Something happened. Chance and Aubrey are taking care of Finn. I need for you to get in the car so I can drive the both of us to the hospital, I'll explain later. Come on, get in."

"I need to go," Eddie tells Yates as he gets into my car. "I'll call later."

"Your phone is dead and charging inside, remember?" Yates states.

"Dude. I have a phone, he'll call later," I snap and already have the car in reverse.

I drive away and head for the hospital. A few minutes pass when Eddie suddenly whispers, "Is she okay? Is she still alive?"

Maggie is the only family he has left and with me mentioning the mere information, he knows very well this is about his mother.

I keep my eyes on the road but reach for his hand and give it a squeeze. "She still had a heartbeat when they put her in the ambulance. I don't know anything else. We'll be there soon, okay?"

He doesn't say anything else but gives my hand a quick squeeze in return before I have to put my hand back on the wheel. Time seems to drag on while we drive over, park the car, and get inside to ask where Maggie was brought to.

We're sitting in the waiting room in silence for

about twenty minutes until a doctor strolls inside and holds his hand out to Eddie and introduces himself and asks, "You're Mrs. Barhamer's son I presume?"

"Yes," Eddie says as he takes the doctor's hand. "How is she doing? What happened?"

"We're still waiting on some results to rule out certain conditions and we are monitoring her closely. The results we are waiting on can explain why your mother had a sudden drop of heart rate and blood pressure which caused her to pass out. At this point we are trying to rule out cardiac conditions. We will keep her here overnight and when all the results have come back we will fully brief you about her condition."

"Can we see her?" I ask and bite my bottom lip right after. I'm intruding. I'm not even family and I shouldn't be here.

The doctor keeps looking at Eddie when he says, "You can go in and see her for a few minutes but she needs to rest."

He holds out his arm to lead the way and Eddie follows him. I have no clue what to do. My feet are rooted to the floor and somehow Eddie notices and steps back to snatch my hand and drag me with him.

When we get inside the room and see Maggie lying in a bed surrounded by equipment, wires, and beeping sounds, it's Eddie who is rooted to the floor this time. I squeeze his hand and make him follow me to the bed. Maggie is sleeping and since the doctor mentioned she needed to rest we're being as quiet as possible.

I place my other hand on Maggie's and lean in to tell her, "You gave us a huge scare, Maggie. Don't do it again. Get better soon, so we can have some tea on the patio. You hear me? We need you." My voice cracks at the end and a sob slips past my lips.

Eddie wraps an arm around my waist and pulls me close. He places a kiss on the top of my head and addresses his mother as he too lowers his voice. "Love you, Mom. Get some rest to get your strength back. The doc told us we need to leave but we'll be back soon, okay?"

He reaches out and lets his knuckles brush over her cheek. Eddie lets me go and steps closer to his mother to place a kiss on her forehead. He murmurs some words in her ear and I watch how his throat bobs as he swallows hard.

"Come on, we need to leave," he croaks and clears

his throat.

I nod warily and follow him out of the room. When we get to the car Eddie takes the keys from my hands and slips into the driver's seat. For a split second I remind myself I should be the one driving, but I guess what happened to Maggie hit us both hard and we just function on autopilot.

My mind suddenly does come to life when Eddie drives up to the gate of his MC and punches in a code. I'm not going inside; he doesn't need to unlock the gate because I'm going home. I start to sputter and think of what to say but he's already parking the car.

I dash out of the car and rush around to face him. "What are we doing here? I need to go home."

"I need to handle a few things here, and I can't go home now or I'll just rip my mind out thinking about my mother. And I need to know you're safe and I won't know for sure unless you're right here with me. Rush might have been arrested and not walking the streets, but his three buddies are out there. If they want to hurt me, they will take you, and I can't let that happen."

"I don't need to tell you I have connections, right? Didn't you hear Yates? He basically implied it's the whole reason you gave me that stupid old lady title. So, just let those idiots know all it was is a title, there's nothing between us. So, excuse me, I'm leaving. And besides, I have to go to pick up Finn because he's staying with two complete strangers for me and for him." Spinning around, I bump right into a hard chest. "Ouch, dammit," I snap, and see it's Yates. "You really need some social skills, peckerwood."

Yates snorts a laugh. "Sorry, doll, that's never going to work. But I'm hoping you're going to stick around to point out the errors of my ways. You being the Pres' old lady and all. And I'm going to start with offering you my apology because I'm a dick. A big one that didn't think and wanted to lash out to Rush how we had the upper hand with you at our side. It came out wrong. When I met Eddie earlier today, he said he had an old lady. And when I asked who, and heard it was you...I was the one who told him he needed to ask your half-brother for help because he would because of you. So, you see, he already claimed you before everything was set into motion. He really does care about you. As a person. Not your contacts, name, whatever...you."

"Right." I roll my eyes. "Nice try. If he said he claimed me first, how the hell did you know who my half-brother was, huh? It's all a load of crap. My life is a load of crap. This whole world is crap." My voice is shaking and tears are streaming down my face.

Yates winces and says, "Eddie? I think you better hold her because I'm pretty sure I broke her, and I don't know how to fix it because everything I say is coming out wrong."

Eddie smacks Yates on the back of his head before he takes me in his arms. "She's not broken you idiot; she's consumed with emotions. All the stuff going on in her life and add what happened at the clubhouse, and now my mother in the hospital. She just needs to catch her breath so back the fuck off."

"I need to get Finn. I'm okay," I mutter through my sobs and try to push away from Eddie.

He feels so right but in the turmoil of everything I don't know what's right or wrong anymore.

"No, you're not okay, darlin'. Come on, let me get you some water and we will take a moment to catch our breath and decide what to do." Eddie doesn't give me a choice but guides me into the clubhouse.

"Rhett, give the lady some water," Yates bellows. "Hudson, make some room."

Bikers left and right move out of the way and act as if I'm in dire need of all the help they can give. A glass of water is being offered from my left and tissues from my right. And there's a hand holding out a piece of chocolate.

I follow the arm that's offering the piece of candy and see it belongs to a rough looking biker with reddish hair and a long beard. I can't really tell how old he is, if I'd have to guess I would go with early thirties.

The chocolate doesn't look chewed and his fingers look clean. Who cares, with the stuff going on in my life, who the hell cares about germs? I reach out and take the piece of chocolate and put it into my mouth. I swear the guy is now sporting the biggest grin on his face, as if I gave him the world by picking what he offered.

I have to close my eyes to savor the sweetness. "Damn, this is so good."

"I know," the redhead rumbles and pulls the rest of the chocolate bar from his back pocket and hands it over.

I greedily take it and ask, "Aren't you scared it'll melt if you have it stashed there?" I ungracefully shove another piece into my mouth.

Laughter rumbles from his throat. "Nah, I just grabbed it when you guys came into the clubhouse. I was going to eat it right away and once I start, I don't stop until I've eaten it all. It's like you blink and it's gone."

"Oh, I know about the blinking, gone instantly but then it will reappear because it will add a few pounds that will never go away. It mainly settles on my ass and thighs, but you don't seem to have that problem." I sigh and still eat another piece of chocolate knowing I will regret it later.

"I happen to like those curves on you," Eddie whispers in my ear and it makes me shiver.

"All right, you guys, give her some room," Eddie says and scoops me up.

"Pres, I've cleaned up the first room on the left for you," a guy says from behind me.

Eddie mutters a thanks and stalks to a room someone from our left opens for us. Once inside he puts me down and locks the door behind us.

Eyeing the movement, I raise my eyebrow. "This was your brilliant plan? Get your brothers to help you distract me to calm me down so you can swoop me away and lock me in here?"

The corner of his mouth twitches. "Nah, I could have thrown you over my shoulder and do just that at any time. My brothers going crazy to make sure you're okay was all them. A little over the top if you ask me, but, yeah. They're good guys," he says and releases a deep sigh.

"You've missed them," I state.

His head slowly bounces up and down. "Yates told me some of the things that went down when I was away. Guys going head to head and not having each other's back. I was afraid Rush killed the spirit of this MC. But this little show of support made me aware he didn't."

"It would really suck if I would grow to like you more and more and then find out you in fact did use me in the end," I grumble, getting tired of this whole situation, and I feel like I should address the head of the snake, so to say.

"I like you. I want you. It has nothing to do with

your name or who you're connected to. Yes, it was one hell of a convenience with the whole Rush situation, but you know damn well how fucking perfect you felt against me last night. That shit isn't something you fake or happens when you want to get off. You burn my insides every time that lush body of yours rocks against me. The need to bury myself deep in you is overwhelming and if I didn't give a fuck then my dick would have taken your tight pussy yesterday. But I didn't."

How on Earth did we get from questioning if it's real between us to discussing last night's non-screw moment? I should question if he thinks he deserves a medal due to the effort he put in there to restrain himself, but like I said...I'm getting tired of this whole situation.

"I want something real, Eddie, and I'm not afraid to say I'm not looking for just sex or a relationship because it's convenient. I want something long-term and meaningful. There's a lot of stuff going on in my life and a lot in yours too. Hell, you're just taking your life back and I absolutely understand your body and mind are occupied and you're trying to balance all of it.

Believe me, I know how overwhelming things can be." I rub a hand over my neck in an effort to release some tension.

Eddie turns me around and presses his fingers against my shoulders, working his way to my neck and shoulder blades. Damn, that feels good. I groan and tilt my head to allow him the room to massage my neck but instead his lips caress my skin.

"I walked out of that prison with only vengeance on my mind and then you stumbled into my life filling my head with endless possibilities to enjoy life to the fullest. Everything might have fallen into place with the people tied to you but that's all it really was, things finally falling into place and moving forward the way it should. I claimed you. You're mine. Not to clear up issues at hand or to benefit myself or others. I'm honest enough to admit I'm a selfish fuck when it comes to you because all I care about is having you next to me, under me, with me at all times. And my fucking chest tightens at the thought of something happening to you, I couldn't bear it and this tells me the feelings you flared up inside me are meant to act on and let them grow because no other woman has awoken something inside me enough to claim as mine, only you."

Okay, then.

The way he stares at me, allowing me to see the honesty in his gaze makes me shiver. I don't have any words to give him in return. Leaning forward I gently brush my lips over his. He growls low in his throat and cups my face to crash his mouth against mine. Consuming. Rough, and yet so caring. He makes me forget why I was questioning our connection in the first place.

If he's selfish, then I can be too, and I'll share his statement... all I care about is having him next to me, under me—with me—at all times.

CHAPTER NINE

EDDIE

In a world swirling every second with insanity it's in this moment where everything is turned off and my body is turned on by the single person engulfing me with her warmth. Kissing this woman gives me pulses of lust, of longing, of righteousness that she belongs to me.

My hands slide down her body and I pull her close, I need her to feel what she does to me. She whimpers and my strength to hold back shatters. It's either dry hump the fuck out of her or bury myself deep. It's not really a hard decision to make. Wait. Dry hump. Finn.

I regretfully tear my mouth away from hers and connect our foreheads. "Where did you say Finn was?"

"Oh, gosh, Finn. I told you I needed to head home. I couldn't leave him with Travis because he is allergic but then Chance and Aubrey showed up. You know, the ones you made me call Travis about to make a reservation. They offered to take care of Finn. You know them, right? And it's not like I had a choice. I needed to get to the hospital and tell you and you weren't answering your phone."

"My phone died when I was calling you. I'm sorry for the whole fuckup and dragging you into this." Dammit.

My throat clogs up and I grab her head to guide it against my chest. I don't have any more words and I can't have her look at me right now because the emotions running inside me are too raw and intense. With my mother in the hospital, it's hitting me hard.

Her arms circle around my waist and she rubs her cheek against my chest. "I'm sure it will all work out. And your mother is a strong woman, she's going to be ordering us around again in no time at all."

"Yeah," I croak.

"We need to get home so I can pick up Finn. I'm sure your friends had other things in mind when they got here than babysit a dog." Gracy steps away from me and I let her.

"My home is here now, Gracelynn. I can't take over and disappear on these guys again. I have to get back to the hospital later too. Fuck." I rub a hand over my face and think of the best way to handle this.

Gracy's hand slides over my chest and it settles right over my beating heart. "Why don't we head over to the estate, say hi to your friends so we can pick up Finn. It will also allow us a chance to pack a bag for your mother because she's going to need a few things since they are keeping her overnight. Then I'll get a few things for myself too, and we'll spend the night here. Wait. Finn is welcome here, right? Am I welcome here?"

She's back in my arms and plastered against my body with my next breath. "Yes. To all. It's the best solution, and why didn't I think about my mother needing me to bring her things? You're perfect, you know that? How you handle everything and step up when needed."

I crash my mouth against hers and relish in the way she drowns me with pleasure coursing through my body. She's my serenity. The eye of the storm where there's a moment of peace in this turmoil they call life.

"Come on, let's go, there's much more I need to handle before we head back to the hospital." I'm about to stalk to the door but the concerned look on her face stops me. "What's wrong?"

"More we need to handle," she murmurs. "I think there's something I need to handle…I'm not sure but it was something Rush said. The whole 'time is ticking, Spencer will have it all' thing he mentioned and how he's working together with Spencer. He would need someone to invest, right? Cough up the cash to fire up his drug business? Well, I left Spencer and everything connected to it behind me almost nine months ago. I'm fairly sure this is about my mother's inheritance because there was an appointment set to go through my mother's will. This is about money, money Spencer will get his hands on, but it belongs to my family, not his. He married my mother for her money and now he's going to get it. Wait. Can he get it if I don't claim it or something? He can't, right? Wouldn't it automatically be mine? I know for a fact my grandfather made Spencer and my mother sign papers before they got married, a prenuptial agreement. I mean, they threw it in each other's face lots of times during many of their fights. I don't know any of this legal stuff, but what I do know is that I have to do something about it to make sure…but what? I have no idea. And I also have zero interest in facing that scumbag." Her shoulders sag and the rambling of words might not make sense to her but it does to me.

"You need to call Clemente. Not because he practically runs this state but because he has the best lawyers. You don't have to go anywhere near Spencer because the lawyer will represent you."

Gracy groans. "Clemente is pissed at me for choosing you, and now you want me to call him so he can do me a favor? Great."

I cup her face and soften my voice. "You have to understand that family holds more meaning to Clemente than it would to anyone else. He would see it as an honor to handle this for you. Hell, I know for a fact he'd be pissed if you would keep this from him."

The storm of emotion clouding her eyes as she

reaches for her phone is hitting me in the chest.

I take the phone from her hands and tell her, "Let me make the call for you."

She nods warily and I tap a few buttons and find Clemente's number. He picks up on the second ring. "Clemente, it's me, Eddie. Listen. Rush implied a few things when he was dragged off and it made Gracy think that Spencer might have something in the works to get his hands on her mother's inheritance. Could something like this be possible? Can you get her a lawyer and find out what's going on? Oh, and I'm ratting her out to you. She's going to be angry with me for telling you this, but she thinks you're pissed at her. She also was under the impression you wouldn't be happy if she called you to do her a favor."

I'm holding the phone at a safe distance from my ear because Clemente is throwing out one curse after the other. Gracy's eyes are wide from shock and I give her a smile and a wink before I give my attention back to the phone call.

"Yeah, Clemente, I mentioned to her what family means to you. I might not have used the shit you just threw out because I respect my old lady." A chuckle slips from my mouth when Clemente adds some more curses but he calms down and thanks me for reaching out but asks me to put Gracy on the phone.

I hold it out for her to take and when Clemente starts to talk, I can see the concern slipping out of her. Clemente will make sure to handle this for her, one way or the other. The man has some issues himself with Spencer so I'm pretty sure he's rubbing his hands with glee to finally have something to sink his teeth in.

Gracy ends the call and tucks her phone away. A sigh of utter relief rips from her body. "He made me promise to call him right away next time. You were right. And he's not angry at me, or at you for that matter, because he appreciated the way you stood up and called him for me. It's just so weird. I was alone for such a long period of time with just my job to fuss about. And really, there's nothing to fuss about because I love running the estate with your mom and living with her. Shit. I hope she's going to be okay and can come home soon, I already miss her so much."

"Come on, let's get going and handle everything so we can check up on her, okay?" I tell her and take her hand.

We stroll back into the main room of the clubhouse and I make sure to grab my phone from the charger.

I'm about to leave when Yates is suddenly standing in front of me. "I just got word Rush made bail. I don't know how, but he's out. Fuck. He shouldn't even have made bail, the damn DEA is involved and the charges were serious enough. He would have had to go before a judge and our criminal justice system doesn't work that fast. You know that as well as I do. Anyway, I had a prospect keeping an eye out and he let me know he walked right out of the precinct, got in a limo, and it drove off. He's following the limo as we speak."

I smack his upper arm. "You did good. My money is on Spencer. He roams around big player, high-class people and might have pulled a few strings to speed things up to let him make bail."

My mind is still running overtime with what I should do when the phone in my hand starts to ring. It's Clemente.

"I just heard. He's out, right?" I grunt into the phone.

"Spencer bailed him out. But listen, that fucker has been living off Gracy's money. There are three more days left before he will receive her mother's inheritance since Gracy signed some papers stating she wants to disclaim it. I hardly think she would do such a thing and my lawyers are already on it to retrieve the original documents to see if the fucker forged her signature and filed without her knowing."

I connect my gaze with Gracy's because I damn well know Clemente is right. "Did you sign any papers before you left Spencer?"

Gracy looks confused and shakes her head, so I ask her again to make sure. "You didn't file any papers to refuse your inheritance?"

Her eyes grow wide at my question before they narrow and anger starts to burn. "I would never do that," she snaps.

"I heard that," Clemente growls. "We're on it and I will let you know once we have all the information."

I make sure to thank him and disconnect, sliding my phone into my pocket right after. "Clemente is handling it. This was exactly what Rush was talking about. Spencer getting the inheritance and having the big cash for investing in the drug dealing business they wanted to run together. Lightners also have a huge chunk of business when it comes to port logistics. Who knows, they might have struck a deal with a cartel or some shit, making it even bigger than we thought it was. Yates, make sure the prospect stays on his ass. We need to know Rush's every move, but let him keep enough distance not to be seen. We're risking a lot as it is. For now, Rush only wants me gone because he will have the MC for manpower and the ability to run his dirty business. I kicked him out, and Spencer might have paid his bail but if they don't have the MC it's just two assholes with a load of cash. Cash he wants to obtain through Gracy. And maybe they also have transportation, but no manpower or backup. Seeing Clemente is working with his lawyers to take away Spencer's money, that wasn't even his in the first place, they might have nothing left to live for and that's when things will get even more dangerous, get me?"

"I fucking get you, brother. We need to have a meeting, get all the brothers up to speed about things. And it might be good to double up, no solo shit because you might think it's just Spencer and Rush but those fuckers have people around them who support them. The cartel supplying the drugs for instance, who knows they might also supply backup because the MC was divided about getting into drugs before you stepped back into the picture and took over. I've seen with my own eyes how Rush and his three buddies have met a few times with what I presume were contacts from a cartel. I know because I've followed them twice to see what they were up to. And these fuckers are armed to the teeth, Pres. What if they have their back?"

"You're right. Fuck," I grumble and think things through.

"We have to get Finn, our dog," Gracy tells Yates. "And we need to pack a bag to take to the hospital later for Eddie's mom. Can someone go with us so we can drive to and from the estate? Then you guys can have your meeting and we'll head to the hospital right after." Gracy's voice sounds timid but she's right and again stepping up when I need her to.

Yates gives her a smile before his gaze slides to me. "Only a few hours with the old lady status and she's already stepping up to the title. I'll have Rhett follow you and while you're handling everything I will make sure to round everyone up for a meeting when you get back."

I'm about to step away but Gracy leans into Yates and asks, "What's the name of the guy with the red hair and beard?"

"Rooney," Yates chuckles. "You want to know where he got the chocolate from, don't ya? I can tell you, it's his, he's the mastermind behind that bar of chocolate. It took him a long time but it's all set and in production. The fucker has made his first million this year. But don't tell anyone I told you because he keeps shit quiet. He only shared it with me because I'm good with numbers and helped him out by reading through contracts he needed to sign to get his product on the market. If Rush knew…he would have made Rooney sell his company to the club. That motherfucker would have wrapped his fat fingers around his throat and would have forced him to sign it over, I just know it."

Gracy reaches out and grabs Yates' forearm. "I'm glad Rooney trusted you and that you stood up for him. Rush will get what's coming to him, we'll make sure he won't be able to interfere with anyone's life."

Yates gives her a nod but the look he gives me is one where he yet again lets me know this woman was made to be the president's old lady. I wrap my arm around her waist and tuck her underneath my arm.

"Rhett," I bellow. "You're with me today."

Rhett dashes up and stalks over to where we're standing. "Ready when you are, Pres."

"See you in about an hour, two tops, Yates," I grunt and head for Gracy's car.

I would rather have her on the back of my bike but we also need to get a few things for my mother and take Finn with us. Within a few minutes we're at the estate and I check with Travis to see which bungalow Chance and Aubrey are staying in.

I've asked Rhett to stay close because there's no need for him to tag along into the bungalow when we get Finn. Not to mention it will raise questions when I bring him along and I don't want to explain or drag Chance into the mess of things. I asked him to come here to take his girl for some relaxing time at the beach, and not to be bothered with my shit.

The door swings open and Chance is in the doorway, holding Finn. The little trouble maker starts to squirm in his arms and he quickly puts him down so he can dash off to Gracy. Figures. He might be my dog, but if I was him, I'd be running into her arms too.

"Hey, Eddie. Everything okay with your mum?" He steps aside so we can enter the bungalow.

I rub my neck and say, "She had a sudden drop of heart rate and blood pressure which caused her to pass out. They're doing some checks and we're headed back to the hospital later. They're keeping her overnight."

Chance nods and I know he's thinking about his own mother. He lost her when he was in prison and didn't even get a chance to say goodbye.

"She's going to pull through," I croak and clear my throat. "I'm sorry I can't stay for a chat."

"No, we completely understand. Let me know how she's doing, mate."

"Will do," I grunt and am about to leave but Aubrey rushes toward us. "Here, don't forget his little friend."

Chance snickers. "Friend? More like fuck buddy. You have a weird dog."

I shake my head while the corner of my mouth twitches. "Says the man who owns a goat."

"Touché," Chance says, giving me a grin right after.

We say our goodbyes and Gracy and I head for my mother's bungalow to grab a few things. Rhett is coming inside this time and is watching how Finn is humping his stuffed animal, a pig this time.

He slowly turns his head toward me. "Is he okay?"

"The dog or the pig?" I snicker.

Finn is completely out of breath but this is his normal and it will make him tired enough to sleep for an hour or two.

"Eddie, can you come here for a sec?" Gracy questions and I stroll over to where she's standing.

She's holding some papers along with an envelope and I'm about to question her when she says, "Let's go into the bedroom so you can help me pick some of the stuff we need to bring with us for your mother."

Gracy doesn't wait for a reply but heads into the bedroom. I follow her and she closes the door behind me, leaning against it the next second while holding out the papers for me to take. "What if Maggie was going through these papers and it triggered something? Could that be possible? Look, there's a little note and it's not your mother's handwriting. I don't recognize whose handwriting it might be."

"It's my father's," I grunt and am frozen to the floor because the papers she's holding are those I recognize all too well and yet I now notice they are slightly different.

I can tell because I recognize the address and it's from the huge mall that's involved with the reason I was sent to prison. Brazen fraud, and I knew someone screwed with the papers because everything was legal and up and running, there was no fucking fraud.

My chest is rising and falling and my heart is beating out of control. Why does my mother have these papers? Papers like this should be in the safe at the office. But it's too much of a coincidence for these papers to be here.

I swallow hard and glance over the documents I've seen before and yet these are different. The note from my father. This. If I had this when I was arrested, I would have walked out a second later because this right here proves my innocence, while at the same time it proves my father's death wasn't an accident but murder. Because him having this is a huge bullseye of motive for someone to kill him to keep things quiet.

CHAPTER TEN

GRACY

"Are you okay?" I whisper.

His whole face went white when he glanced over those papers he's holding. They don't make any sense to me but the way they were all spread out on the table it looked like Maggie was reading them and needed some fresh air. That's probably why I found her on the patio instead of inside the house.

"I knew that fucker was behind everything," Eddie mutters and grabs his phone. He waits a few breaths before he starts to rattle, "Clemente, did your lawyer get your hands on those documents they said Gracy signed?"

Eddie throws the papers he was holding on the bed and starts to stalk back and forth as he listens to whatever Clemente is telling him.

"I have something I want to compare it with because I have a gut feeling. Yeah. The clubhouse. Okay. An hour, see you there." He hangs up and grabs his head as he tips it back.

I'm almost afraid to breathe because the way he's acting? My hunch about this being the thing that led to his mother ending up in the hospital is true. I mean, if Eddie is reacting this way, it must be very bad. It pains me to see him like this.

I take a deep breath and repeat the question, "Are you okay?"

Eddie slowly drops his hands and his gaze collides with mine. The torment raging through him is intense.

"No," he growls and he's standing before me with my next breath.

He takes my lips in a raw kiss and the way his tongue is swirling against mine makes me gladly submit to his dominance.

His mouth is ripped away and right next to my ear

as he says on a hot breath, "I need to feel you wrapped around me. You're the one thing keeping me grounded. The only good that entered my fucked-up life. Say yes, Gracelynn."

How can I ever resist when the feelings he just shared with me could have been voiced by myself?

"Yes," I gasp when he rolls his hips, allowing me to feel his hard length pressing against my belly.

A growl rumbles through his chest and he pulls slightly back to create space between us. He starts to tug at my jeans and it makes me reach out to do the same to him but it takes too much effort.

Frustration makes me snap, "You do yours, I do mine. Shit. You better have a condom."

He reaches for his back pocket and holds out a foil package.

"Yes!" I breathe as I kick away my jeans and underwear while throwing my top over my head and onto the floor.

I'm left in just my bra while Eddie is still dressed. Well, his zipper is down and his jeans are hanging onto his hips and he has his fingers wrapped around his huge, hard dick as he slowly slides up and down.

He rips the foil package with his teeth and easily slides the condom on.

"Gosh, that's sexy," I whisper, mainly to myself.

There's a rumble in his chest before he's on me. My back is pressed to the wall behind me and my ass is in his hands as he lifts me up, allowing me to wrap my legs around his waist.

"Sorry, darlin'," Eddie grunts. "First round is going to be hard and rough."

As if I would file a complaint. "Just get inside me already because I've never felt this empty and wet and you're the only one who can do something about it."

He reaches between us and aligns his dick with my pussy, sliding it back and forth and coating himself with my juices. Sweet heaven, if he keeps this up, I will come without having him inside me.

He enters me with just the tip and if I thought he was big when I looked at it, it feels like a monstrosity now. He buries his head in the crook of my neck, his hot breath spreading over my skin and the grunts coming from his mouth is making sparks of electricity dance through my body.

This is not just sex, this is an intimate connection,

a driven need to devour one another. I slide my arms underneath his leather cut and let my nails trail up and down his back. Even through the fabric of his shirt he loves the feel and it makes him slide fully inside me in one hard thrust.

I'm gasping for my next breath as Eddie starts to pound inside me. By now I'm consumed by this man and can only fist the fabric of his shirt to hold on. The pleasure building inside my body is bound to explode any second.

His fingers are gripping my ass, his mouth is sucking my neck, and the way he switches up the angle of his thrusts so he grazes my clit is making me scream his name as my pussy starts to convulse around his dick.

The way he says my name on a hot breath as it flows over into a rough grunt is making my body shake with a bonus orgasm as tribute. Hot damn, I don't think I've ever had such a raw connection with someone. Eddie is struggling for his next breath and so am I. I can feel him soften inside me and when he slightly shifts, he slides out, making the both of us groan.

"Way too fucking short," Eddie mutters.

And all my mind offers in reply is, "Most definitely not talking about his dick."

The way Eddie bursts out a laugh makes me aware I've said it out loud. He's still chuckling when he strolls into the bathroom to get rid of the condom. I take this time to quickly put my clothes back on and I'm done the second Eddie walks back into the room.

This after sex thing, papers scattered on the bed, Maggie in the hospital, Spencer, Rush, the whole she-bang is making me question how to act or what to say but it seems Eddie takes over when he stalks right up to me and wraps his fingers around the back of my neck to pull me close.

I expect the kiss to be raw and hard but he sur-prises me by giving me gentleness. Our lips are caught in a sensual dance and it makes me want to throw my clothes back on the floor. He pulls away too soon for my liking and gives me an intense stare as if he's checking to see if I'm okay.

"I'm going to need to handle a few things in the up-coming hour but you're going to be by my side every second, understood? Those papers behind me are proof of my innocence and if they get into the wrong hands,

I can't put the one responsible behind bars. Hell, maybe it's more than one person if my suspicions are correct and it would also add murder to it. Because this also is proof my father, along with Nicolaus, Rush's father, were murdered by Rush."

Eddie takes a moment to expel a breath or two, as if he's contemplating what he should tell me or keep to himself, before he continues. "Nicolaus and my father's functions were more the overseeing kind. Make decisions, take on new projects, visit potential investors, that sort of thing. Except, the night they died they were standing on top of a building that we handled the renovations for. The police ruled their deaths as an unfortunate accident. Something about floors not being safe and it gave way causing them to fall to their death. But neither of them should have been there. These papers?" Eddie's voice is an angry growl and he swallows hard, as if to catch himself losing control and is trying to calm himself down.

He glances back at the bed and points. "These papers shine a whole new light on what went down that night. And I know for a fact Rush didn't just shove me out of the way so he could take over the club, this has been going on for a while to gather funds for his drug dealing ambitions. I might have pulled you into this but the papers lying behind me are the real documents while the forged ones were the ones that got me convicted. And with Spencer forging documents and working with Rush, I'm thinking those two have been working together for years. I don't know the finer details yet, but I'm going to find out. By doing so I might open a can of worms where there's no turning back from. I can't promise your safety and maybe it's better if you move in with Clemente for a few days, or as long as it takes for me to solve this. And I might have to put someone at the hospital to keep an eye on my mother because I'm pretty damn sure she didn't know she had this and my mind is still boggling over the fact these papers were in her possession, and I'm wondering how she got them. See? It's all a fucking mess and I don't know where to start."

"You start by facing one thing at a time. And you're not going to send me away like a little child. All of this involves me too. I'm here, I can help. Let me help. And you know as well as I do that you have a solid partner in Clemente if—"

"If I keep you safe because if something happens to you, I'm sure my next breath will be my last. That's why I suggested you could stay with him, let us work this out. Because I also can't focus if I'm not sure you're safe," Eddie tries again.

It's not going to work; I've made up my mind. Besides, I need to do this, not just for him, but for me. "I ran away from Spencer once and ignored everything to pick myself up and start over. Look what that got me. Almost losing my mother's family's legacy to a man who never loved my mother but wanted her money instead. And he might be getting it too. I'm done ignoring things and not stepping up for what's right. So, you forget about stashing me away because I'm not going to leave your side, understood?"

"You're right," Eddie says with determination now evident in his voice. "How badly I want to keep you out of this, it's not possible because you're connected to all of this too. Come on, we have to pack a bag for my mother and get back to the clubhouse. I need to talk things through with Clemente first before I get my brothers up to speed. Then we'll drop the bag off at the hospital and hopefully get some good news."

"I'm sure she'll be awake when we get there, and if she's not, you know it's for the best that she rests up to regain her strength. And maybe those papers made a huge impact on her and explains why her body reacted this way. We have to stay positive for now until we know more. One thing at a time, remember?"

The corner of his mouth twitches. "Mr. and Mrs. Positive, huh?"

"You know it," I quip. "Go grab those papers and tuck them away safely. I'll head into the other bedroom and grab a few things for her."

I turn on my heels and head for the door but Eddie snatches my hand and makes me glance back.

"You're really something, Gracelynn," he murmurs. "A reason to live beyond the need for justice to prevail. I'm one lucky man to have such a good thing in my life. A strong woman who doesn't let anyone interfere with what she wants."

My chest blooms with warmth. "Save the sweet talk for later, pretty boy. Because saying things like that will get you laid and we don't have the time...we have work to do."

He barks out a laugh and tries to keep from smiling

big. "Yes, ma'am," he finally says and heads for the bed to snatch up all the papers.

It takes me a few minutes to grab what I need from the other bedroom and I hear Eddie throw a question at Rhett as he steps from the patio into the living room. "What were you doing out there?"

"I had to get some fresh air, Pres," Rhett groans. "You and your old lady were getting it on in the bedroom and the dog takes after the owner because he's rubbing one out on a stuffed animal while I'm here twiddling my thumbs. Yeah, stepping out there and enjoying the ocean view seemed like the right thing to do."

My cheeks heat when I hear Rhett mention he heard me and Eddie having sex, but his ramblings right after make me giggle. I place Maggie's bag in the hallway and enter my own bedroom to pack myself a bag because we're going to be staying at the clubhouse. With everything going on and Eddie being the president of Unruly Defenders MC, that's where he needs to be.

I make sure to bring Finn's bowls and food so everyone is set for at least a few days. We all head out and a few minutes later we're walking into the clubhouse.

It's crowded and Yates comes rushing toward us to take the bowls and Finn's food out of my hands.

"Where do you want me to put them?" he questions.

"My room. I'm not trusting Finn running around here when I'm handling things so he can sleep, eat, and stay in our bedroom when we need to do other things and can't bring him along," Eddie tells him.

"Smart," Yates quips. "But I'm sure the little dude is going to fit right in. It's all of the others who need to adjust to having a dog around. And an old lady, let's not forget Gracy is the first old lady of this MC's new generation. You're moving in too, right, Gracy?"

I have to swallow a few times at the dryness in my mouth to form a word, and I'm glad I don't have to because Eddie is answering for me.

"Are you seriously stealing my thunder, VP? I was thinking of having her hang around here for a few days and letting the guys and the place grow on her before popping the question." Eddie shakes his head and hardens his tone. "If she runs away, I'm blaming you."

Yates' eyes slide to me and they widen as crinkles appear in his forehead. He holds his fingertips in front of his mouth and by doing this he's clearly saying "Oops," without words and it makes me smile big. The mischief dancing in his eyes makes him appear ten years younger and I have to say, he makes me feel at ease.

"Don't worry, Yates, I'm not going anywhere. Well, not without Eddie." I shoot him a wink and head for the room we were in the last time.

Eddie follows me and we drop our stuff on the bed. I scoop Finn up and it makes me wonder. "Did you mention we were leaving Finn here? In this room or with the guys? Did you need to have the meeting now or are we going to your mother first?"

Rooney pops his head into the room. "I could watch the little doggie for you. I'm going to do some reading so I could be in my room or in the main room, whatever makes you feel at ease but Finn won't be alone, he'd be with me."

"Okay." I give Rooney a grateful smile. "But don't feed him any chocolate."

"No worries. I used to own a Dutch Shepherd. I know how to take care of a dog."

"A man with many talents," I compliment. "Wait,

what else can you do, and did you bring me some more chocolate? I need more. I would love to pay for them too."

Rooney steps inside the room and lowers his voice. "I'm testing some new stuff. One of those is vanilla truffle with a twist of caramel. I could use a test subject if you're offering."

"Hells yes," I squeak and add, "I'm never going to leave you guys ever again. Well, I probably can't in a few months of testing, my ass will be too big to fit through the door with all the chocolate I'm going to stuff into my mouth."

Rooney snickers, "From what Rhett mentioned, Pres here will make sure to burn those calories right off."

Eddie growls low in his throat.

"I'm outta here. Come find me when I need to look after Finn, and I'll have some chocolate for you, 'kay?"

"Thanks Rooney," I quip and have to smile at Eddie's reaction, being all protective while Rooney was only joking around.

Earlier at the house I was slightly embarrassed when Rhett mentioned he heard me and Eddie having sex. And with Rooney mentioning it I know these guys are all close friends. A bunch of dirty gossip, teenage level, bachelors. But I have a feeling I'm going to fit right in, because they all seem nice, supportive, and caring. I can see why Eddie is fighting hard for this place and those brothers along with it.

"Let's head over to the hospital first, I'll postpone the meeting. I hope my mother is awake since I need to ask her where she got the papers from," Eddie says, rubbing a hand over his neck and he looks so tired.

"Let's go, hopefully we'll get some good news about her, and the papers." I take his hand and give a little tug to get him moving.

I grab both the stuffed animal and Maggie's bag with my other hand along the way. We walk into the main room and I notice Rooney is sitting next to Hudson at the bar. I bend down to scoop Finn up and hand him over to Rooney.

"He's in your care now. Don't let him slip out of the front door and if you want him to sleep, give him this." I thrust the stuffed animal in his lap and Finn starts to squirm to get it.

Rhett starts to laugh and snatches up the stuffed

animal. "You guys go ahead, I'll watch Finn and Rooney. I'll show everyone else Finn's neat trick." He ushers us away and starts to explain. "Check it out, you know the whole statement how the dog takes after the owner? And how Pres walked out of prison, stepping in here with an old lady attached to his arm? Look." Rhett throws the stuffed animal on the floor and takes Finn from Rooney, placing him on the floor. Finn heads straight for the stuffed animal and starts to hump.

"For fuck's sake, this is why Finn stayed at my mother's most of the time," Eddie mutters while laughter fills the clubhouse.

"Come on, I need to head out of here with these teenage fucks with one-track minds," Yates grumbles before he raises his voice. "Ash, tag along. We need eyes on our Pres' mother, that's you."

The four of us head out and I'm hoping with all my heart we will get some positive news about Maggie. And hopefully Eddie will get an answer about where the papers and the envelope came from.

— CHAPTER ELEVEN —

EDDIE

I'm listening to the doctor's ramblings but nothing is making sense because I'm not paying attention. When we arrived at the hospital and were about to go into my mother's room, the doctor stopped us and wanted me to answer a few questions.

First question? Did my mother endure any extreme pressure or does she have any underlying stress? Naturally my thoughts went straight to the papers and everything else faded to the background.

"Could you please rephrase what you just mentioned? I'm not sure if I understand completely what happened with all the medical terms," Gracy says, and I'm thankful she's with me.

The doctor nods at Gracy but turns his attention to me again. "We believe your mother had a vasovagal syncope. This caused her heart rate and blood pressure to suddenly drop, which led to reduced blood flow in her brain. It was the reason she lost consciousness. We were worried she might have an underlying medical condition such as a heart or brain disorder. Your mother mentioned she's had a low heart rate all her life, has something like this happened before? Do you know if she endures underlying stress or maybe extreme pressure? Were there recent changes that could have triggered a stressful moment?"

I now know for a fact what happened to my mother was because of the papers Gracy noticed on the table. I don't know where my mother got them from, but it's the damn reason she's in the hospital. More anger hits me because this whole thing that landed me in prison is like a black hole, swallowing everyone around me into this mess.

"She's been missing her husband more and more these days, and Eddie just came back after a long time, and he has been wrapped in some issues. I'm sure as a mother she's worried and maybe it all became too much," Gracy offers because I'm still tongue-tied. "But I also know that she's been more tired the last few months and has made a few changes. Less work, more time to relax. She assured me nothing was wrong with her physically and that it all had to do with getting older one day at a time. Should we have been more alert? Should I have forced her to go to the doctor? Would it have prevented what happened to her today?"

Everything is running through my head and it's mostly guilt when I hear the last few things Gracy is mentioning. Should I have been more alert too? I can't think of anything to say to mingle in this discussion, mainly because I haven't been around my mother in a while.

And for fuck's sake, what do I even say to this doctor? The truth? I can't even comprehend everything myself. And do I even want to talk to my mother about this while it's probably the reason why she's in this hospital bed? The doctor in front of me offers me his hand and I warily take it. Seems I missed half of the conversation yet again.

Gracy squeezes my hand and says, "Let's go see your mother."

Yates and Ash are waiting across the hall as we enter my mother's room. Like last time there are beeping sounds and machines surrounding her but she's sitting slightly up. The smile she gives us both is warming my chest.

"Hey, Ma," I croak.

She waves me over. "Edgar Augustine, come give your mother a hug. I won't break."

Little does she know my own heart is breaking seeing her like this and knowing what put her in here isn't over and handled yet. It makes me feel even more like a failure. I drag myself over to the bed and carefully hug her. The deep sigh ripping from her body is letting me know the hug is something she gathers strength from.

"Don't ever scare me like that again," I mutter. "I'm not ready to lose you too."

"I'm still here, son. I'm not going anywhere. Well, maybe home soon because I would like to spend the night in my own bed but they have mentioned I needed to stay overnight."

"Yes, they need to keep an eye on you but from my understanding if everything goes well, they will release you tomorrow and Eddie and I will be right here to pick you up. So, you'd better do as ordered and get some rest. And I will make sure you won't have any extra work or stress, you need to take it slow for a while," Gracy says, though she too knows about the papers.

I've never trusted a woman or shared crucial information with one. The world I grew up in was one raised in an MC where brotherhood was strong but crucial information was club business. Things discussed in church aren't meant to be out in the open.

Though, I know very well each club and president have their own little rules, but I know for a fact my father never involved my mother with club business. And yet it doesn't stop her from worrying about all of it. It's the reason I convinced my father that me buying the estate for her was a great way to keep her mind busy.

The little things she did for the construction company weren't really needed and she would always rave about her dream to run a tiny bed and breakfast. Being in the construction and the real estate world along with it, I got wind about the estate becoming for sale.

It cost me almost my whole savings I had gathered through investments, but it was worth it when I saw her face the moment I brought her to the gate and told her it was hers to run and turn into her little paradise.

Though my father was a hard worker and a man of little words, he helped me and my mother after I bought the estate. There was some construction work needed and he took control. And I know it bothered him when I bought the estate but I also knew all his money was wrapped up in his company.

It's always the next job where money is needed to be pumped into, it's the way he's always worked and how we all got to where we were. But I owed them both. Every cent I made was with the help of my father as I worked my way up his company where he gave me all the possibilities.

He allowed me to go through college, get a degree and through working for his company, I made my first paycheck. Due to the MC I could save on everything so I could invest and I was lucky enough it all worked out.

It's the reason I invested it all back into property. The whole needing money to make money was true for me and the reason I was able to have enough to do everything I wanted. Though the estate I bought for my mother was different.

After I bought it, we all decided it was better if it would stay in my name, because my father kept telling us how fragile running a construction company was. Investors failing, market plunging, if I kept it in my name my mother would always keep her dream if something happened to my father's company.

It's also the reason why I bought the MC property and the bar next to it. Both investments and making sure everything was kept in the family. And with the estate being my mother's dream, I know it's not causing her any stress, if anything it's a stress relief because she's mentioned many times how waking up every morning in her bungalow and seeing the view of the ocean sets her mind at peace.

"The estate practically runs itself, it's not what's caused this nor will it cause her the added stress," I grumble. "Ma, it was the papers we found on the table that landed you in here, wasn't it?"

Her whole face falls and the bleeping of the machines starts to change.

"Calm down, Maggie," Gracy says, her tone filled with worry.

"The papers," my mother gasps and grabs my arm. "You need to get them. They can prove you're innocent and there's a note from your father. You need to read it because he wrote down his thoughts about what went wrong with the mall project and how he was heading to meet Rush along with Nicolaus. He confronted Nicolaus earlier that day with the two sets of documents he found and how he saw Nicolaus' son, Rush on camera exchanging them. Your father took the papers out of the container outside where Rush threw them in and put everything in an envelope along with a copy of the video. He needed to know if Nicolaus was in on it too."

My mother furiously shakes her head as her hand tightens into a fist. "William never should have tried to solve it internally like club business. What was he thinking accepting Rush's suggestion to meet up in that building? He should have gone straight to the police with everything he had, and the suspicions. But instead he put it in the safe and went to meet Rush along with Nicolaus. And the note your father wrote clearly states Nicolaus didn't know and didn't believe Rush would do such a thing. It's obvious Rush killed them both. It wasn't an accident; Rush took my William away from me. I didn't know, Eddie. I didn't know this envelope was in the safe all along, and I wouldn't have ever found it if it wasn't for you and Gracy."

Her words thunder through my head. There's a video showing Rush swapped those documents? Clearly, I didn't check inside the envelope well enough, only the documents concerning the investment for a mall project where investors transferred thousands of dollars into a bank account. One of the two versions we now found was in Rush's name and bank account.

But that fucker changed it all when he got caught and made it seem I was the one ripping everyone off. He must have done it in the days after the deaths of our fathers. So, ultimately there were three sets and no one knew about these two my father had safely stashed in his safe…to protect the evidence as he went out to investigate on his own.

I had my suspicions Rush had something to do with

everything. Mainly due to a text I received right before my father left for that meeting where he let me know he needed to talk to me about Rush and the company.

Why the hell didn't my father do things differently? Trusted another person to have his back? Trusted me. I've asked myself these questions many times. Even more because I've been stabbed in the back by one of my own brothers. And now I realize he not only betrayed me, my father, and his own father. But I'm sitting on evidence that gives motive for the murder of my father and his own.

I can't wrap my head around the fact someone wouldn't twist his hand about killing his own father. Over money? Or was Rush deep into something bigger he couldn't get out of? Fuck. It's driving me insane.

"What was it about me and Eddie that made you check the safe?" Gracy questions.

My mother's face turns to my old lady and she gives her a warm, but sad smile. "You two reminded me of William and myself. When Eddie told me he was going to claim you as his old lady it made me want to hold the leather property cut William gave me when I became his old lady. It was in the safe. We put it there many years ago because I didn't have to wear it. In the years of our relationship where he was building up the club I did. It has a patch on the back that says 'Property of Barhamer.' Wearing it made everyone aware who I belonged to, who protected me. Through the years everyone knew and respected me and it made wearing it unnecessary. I wanted to preserve it." Her eyes trail off into the distance and I know her thoughts are with my father.

"I would love to see it," Gracy says, her voice filled with emotion.

My mother's head turns in her direction and she reaches out to stroke Gracy's cheek. "I wanted to give the cut to Eddie so he could give it to you. But when I took it out of the safe, I noticed the envelope lying underneath it."

"I'm going to make everything right," I vow fiercely. "All you need to worry about is getting your strength back so you can enjoy sitting on the patio while watching the waves of the sea caress the beach. Remember the mornings and nights you and dad would spend together."

That's one thing my father did and never let anything or anyone influence that time of day. My mother gives me a radiant smile as she repeats the words my dad used to say. "Sunsets and sunrises are there to remind you of time passed and time to come, a solid promise of life and how the world keeps turning."

"A life shared together and hold strong to embrace a new day," I croak, words my mother used to say to my father in return.

A lone tear slides over her cheek. "Promise me one thing, Eddie."

"Anything," I tell her, my voice a strong promise.

"Don't make the same mistakes your father made. Even if you think you're protecting the ones you love, don't. He never shared club information with me, but in return I never asked. But looking back now…I would have rather carried some of the burdens with him because in the end he thought he needed to take everything on himself. Maybe I'm taking this the wrong way, and with Rush's father involved and Nicolaus being his VP and everything, maybe William felt like he couldn't trust anyone, but I dread this is what got him killed. Gracy is right here, Eddie, and she's strong.

She's been there for me every day since I met her. Don't shut her out, don't shut anyone out and think you can handle everything by yourself."

Through all this turmoil of emotions I feel like I need to lighten the mood. My mother needs it more than anything. This leads me to quip, "I don't need the sales pitch, Ma. I already claimed her and I intend to keep her; sunsets, sunrise, and everything in between while this world keeps on spinning."

Fuck. The way her eyes start to water makes me doubt if this was the right thing to say.

She turns her head to Gracy. "I would like to have grandchildren very soon."

"Ma!" I snap.

My mother chuckles vindictively and says, "It was worth a try to speed things up with me lying in here. I'm not dead yet, son. But, like I said, I would like to have some grandchildren. Embrace what you have. Fully embrace, Eddie."

I understand her underlying tone. And I know she's right and I have been trusting Gracy from the start, even more than others. I've even shared about the papers. We all learn from our mistakes and this is too big to handle for only one person.

I reach out and take Gracy's hand. "I am, believe me, I am."

Gracy gives me a shy smile and now even her eyes are filling with tears. Shit. We need to get out of here before mine start to water.

"Ma, I need to go handle things now. I'm putting a prospect in the hallway to keep an eye on you. If there's anything, holler, okay? We'll come by tomorrow to pick you up so don't start to hit on any sexy doctors because come morning, we're busting you out of here."

She smacks my upper arm but grabs it right after and gives a slight pull. Knowing what she wants I lean in and give her a hug.

"Take my cut from the safe and give it to your old lady, let everyone see who she belongs to."

"Will do, Ma," I tell her, and give her an extra squeeze and a kiss on her forehead.

I take a step back and let my mother hug Gracy. They exchange some hushed words before we leave the room. Yates comes with us while Ash stays behind to keep watch.

I don't expect anyone to come after my mother, but I'm not taking any chances. The three of us head for the clubhouse A black limo is parked in front and when we drive up to the gate and Yates punches in the code, I can see Clemente is sitting in the limo when he slides down the window. He drives up behind us and when Gracy and I get out of the car, he walks up and gives Gracy a hug.

I know they're family but it bugs me to see Gracy in any other man's arms. Crazy and unnecessary but it's just the way my mind works.

"We need to talk," I grunt.

Clemente steps back but stays close to Gracy. "Do you want to discuss everything inside? Or in the checked and safe surroundings of my limo?" Clemente says.

Remembering my mother mentioning the video that caught Rush swapping papers reminds me of technology. Normally I wouldn't think twice about these things but what if someone is listening in on things? Doesn't have to be Rush but Clemente mentioned how there were eyes on Rush and maybe there's a chance we have a rat in the MC, an undercover cop, or a bug planted in church.

Dammit, I have to stop doubting everyone and everything. Even my mother told me not to make the same mistake my father made.

This makes me state, "Limo. But I need Gracy in there too, along with Yates." I turn my attention to my VP. "Yates, give me two names of brothers you would trust blindly."

He's been around this MC when I wasn't and knows what we're up against and what happened in the past. All of this makes him the perfect man to know who we can trust to discuss a plan of action.

"Rooney and Rhett," Yates replies instantly.

And that's just it. No questions whatsoever why I'm asking or what needs to be done, a solid reply without thinking twice.

"Get them. And let the others know we'll be right there to have a meeting with everyone, okay?" Yates nods at my words and heads into the clubhouse.

It doesn't take long for him to return with Rooney and Rhett. All of us get inside the limo.

Rhett whistles low. "Dude, all that's missing is the pink lights in the roof and you'd have a pimpmobile."

The all black leather interior and the minibar in front of the large couch does give the impression a few people can have quite the party in here.

"Shut your mouth, imbecile," Clemente grunts. "A simple pimp couldn't afford this bulletproof vehicle. And there's no way I'd pay women to step inside my limousine."

"Well, excuuuuuuse me," Rhett whispers underneath his breath.

Clemente gives him a glare and connects his eyes with me. "This is how you want to do this?"

It's not hard to miss the undertone. He doesn't like me bringing in others to discuss this. Though, I'm the one in charge. Besides, "I'd rather not do this at all but I see no other way around it."

Gracy places her hand over my thigh and I cover it with mine. Clemente eyes the movement and I know deep down he's still not happy Gracy and I are together.

Without taking the papers out of the pocket of my leather cut, I voice the words, "I have evidence Rush is the one who set me up to rot in jail. And with it a video too, all of it implies he's also responsible for the death of his father and mine."

There's only silence ringing loud. I know Rhett and Rooney know about the accident my father and Rush's father were involved in and they also know I went to jail for brazen fraud.

"The mall project. Rush put it all in my name when he knew it went to shit. I suspect Rush never expected my father and his to find out about what he was doing. Seeing Rush's job was handling the administration parts and no one checked what he did. And for fucking real, how did he ever think to get away with scamming investors out of their money? We're talking about hundreds of thousands here. He forged the papers and made it seem I was the one behind everything. Long story short, I have the original documents along with the ones Rush exchanged them with so the money all went into his back account. He changed them again when it went to shit and we all know they're in my file as the so-called evidence that got me convicted. Because that fucker put my name on it."

I shake my head because even for me all of this sounds confusing so, I add, "In the end there were three versions of the contract but there was only one others knew about. The original one, which was never used, the one with Rush's bank account, and the one that got me convicted. I now own all of them and to make it all complete, there are also a few handwritten notes from my father along with a video. This video shows Rush opening the safe and clearly swapping files, everything points to Rush. Except," I rub a hand over my face and release a deep breath. "For the life of me I can't figure out the motive. What would he need all that money for? He was like me, involved in our father's construction company. Rush had a damn desk job and was making good cash. I know he lived royally and where I invested my money—and was very lucky to be successful with it—he spent it on women and snorting blow but this? I don't get it. And turning everything in won't give me justice for the death of my father or the years I spent behind bars. My gut is telling me this is bigger and I can't wrap my mind around it. I'm missing something and it might all blow back in my face, but…I need clear eyes, ears, and a sane mind to help me take the next step."

More silence greets me until Clemente leans in and places his forearms on his knees. "The day your father died happened about a week before you went to jail? How long ago was that? About two, two and a half years ago, right? I looked into your case; after you were arrested, the money was returned. You made sure of it by selling some of your property. Even if you didn't do it, and never pleaded guilty. Still, you were convicted of felony embezzlement…brazen fraud. The judge might have made an example out of you because of previous embezzlement cases in the months prior by others who were indeed guilty."

I nod slowly. "Rush was also screwing my lawyer, making me feel like the bitch didn't do anything to plead my case and instead got me a higher sentence, even if I changed lawyers. There were several complications. It didn't matter if it was my first offense and the money and bank account was never linked with me, hell…they didn't even exist. Like you said, the judge might have made an example out of me, but it didn't help my case when I punched Rush in the face in front of the courthouse. Everything about my case has been one fuckup. I should be happy I only got the few years along with a reduced sentence because I could have killed that fucker with my bare hands if they gave me a chance."

"I might know Rush's motive for needing a load of cash," Clemente says and his gaze slides from me to Gracy. "Something happened a few years ago. The timeline…it fits."

— CHAPTER TWELVE —

GRACY

Clemente mentions the timeline and it makes me gasp. "That's around the time we met. When your father came back and ran into my mother."

Clemente rubs his fingers over his lips as if he's thinking things through. "What if your mother and my father reconnecting made a wave in your mother's marriage?"

"She was separated from my father a few weeks after they met. I didn't think anything of it at the time, I mean…they were always fighting so my first thought was 'finally!' But what if Rush did work with Spencer and they both forged the papers because they needed the money? Money Spencer needed for himself because my mother left him. Or maybe he invested with Rush and needed it back because my mother found out he took her money? Because I know for a fact my grandfather made sure everything stayed in my mother's name."

"My lawyers were able to get their hands on the papers that were filed to refuse your inheritance. They had them checked and the report stated they were forged." Clemente gives his attention to Eddie. "I'm guessing if we put the papers you're talking about right next to them…maybe they were forged by the same one. Wait. I suddenly remember something. It might be nothing but it's too much of a coincidence." Clemente reaches for his phone and starts to type. "Here."

He turns his phone and both me and Eddie lean in to see a news article about a huge drug bust in one of the nearby ports.

"I checked into Spencer's background and saw he used to be the CEO of a freight and shipping company." Clemente continues, "What if he used to get a golden handshake every now and then to look the other way when it involved certain ships? They could have been working together for a while. And what if they owed a cartel cash for a deal gone wrong?"

"It's like tiny pieces of a puzzle," I mumble to myself. "And if this is true, it's connected to all of us. Crossed paths even before we met. But it also means this isn't as simple as turning in the evidence, Eddie. What if Clemente is right and years ago those drugs that were taken were meant for Rush? Has he paid them off by using the investors' money? Those funds were never retrieved because he faked the bank account he put in your name, right?"

"There was no money," Eddie grunts. "I thought I could escape jail time if I paid off the few investors who had proof they transferred the money. But those funds were transferred to a Swiss bank account, it didn't match the one on the contract. Like I said, there was a lot wrong with my case."

"You were lucky you only spent a few years on the inside and had a reduction in sentence, man. Fuck," Yates grunts.

"Every month Rush drops off a package. I've walked into him putting cash into a leather bag and he either drops it off himself or lets Banjo or Maxton drop it off," Rhett suddenly says. "Is he still paying it off or getting drugs in small portions? I know he was about to drag the whole MC into his business but he never made a secret of his selling drugs on the side, so I never questioned his activity as long as he didn't pull any of us in along with it. But from what I heard Banjo mention a few times when he was drunk off his ass is that Rush only has three big clients and he basically just makes sure he gets the drugs off the boat and transports them to those three and swaps the money. Then the money needs to be dropped off. They make it sound easy and risk free but we all know that shit isn't."

"It's a sales pitch," Clemente tells him. "I don't think Banjo was drunk when he shared that piece of information with you. Nor did you accidentally walk in on seeing Rush with a pile of cash. It sounds more like a way to buy souls. Make you interested in an easy way to earn big cash fast. Gracy, I believe your family owns or co-owns one of the major ports in California, right? And when you think about Spencer who used to be the CEO of a freight and shipping company...

there's a link between all of it all right. I'm sure my father will have more information about what goes on in those ports. I have to talk to him after we're done here and explain everything, he might have more insight with the connections he has. He might also know who Rush is dealing with and if I do, I will put an end to it."

"Can you do that?" I gasp. "Go to a drug dealer or a cartel for that matter…that's what they call these things, right? I mean, those things are huge, and you're saying you can just…shoo them away? I know I make it sound easy but it really sounds unrealistic, all of it."

"It's complicated and it will take some meetings with the right people but it's all about having the necessary contacts and power." Clemente gives her a satisfied grin. "Power comes with order; my family has earned this and is respected. When my father moved to Italy, my uncle took over and when we returned, my uncle retired and it was my time to take over but that shouldn't have happened the way it did. My father would have been in charge for a few more years while I was at his side. But with the death of your mother… your mother. Her death was ruled a suicide, right?"

I swallow hard and can only nod. Even if it's been almost nine months, her sudden death still hits me hard every time I think about it.

"I think it's time I had a little chat with Spencer," Clemente suddenly says and locks eyes with Eddie. "I'm not liking the way this deepens and crosses lives and paths."

"When? 'Cause I want in," Eddie says and there's a look in his eyes I can't place.

My gaze ping pongs between Clemente and Eddie because I don't understand their reasoning. "Aren't we supposed to leave Spencer to the police? I mean, the whole thing with him forging my signature and filing something I didn't…that's fraud and will put him behind bars, right?"

Clemente's face stays the same, not one twitch different, but when I glance at Eddie there's sadness and…pity? For me? Why? And when did this discussion go from my mother to Spencer?

A jolt of awareness fires through my veins making me gasp, "No. You're thinking Spencer killed my mother?"

Oh. My. God. And the worst is…it actually makes

more sense than my mother killing herself because she was clearly happier when they separated and she moved out of Spencer's house.

Eddie wraps his arm around my waist and plasters me against his body. His lips are touching my temple in a tender kiss. "One thing at a time, darlin', one thing at a time."

I lean into his touch to search his strength in all of this. Clemente is holding his phone as if he just contacted someone or is about to but he's watching us instead.

"I'll have him within the hour. Do you need to talk things through with your guys first?"

"Pres." Yates clears his throat. "I'm thinking it would be better to have the meeting later when we have more details. It's a lot to process and if we can iron out more details and get balls rolling ourselves it's better to present the whole thing at once instead of shards of information. Unless we need more manpower."

"I have more manpower." Clemente grins. "And I second your VP's thoughts. Besides, I also put out a few feelers to see who Rush's supplier might be and where Rush might be hiding out."

"I know for a fact he owns a building near Monrovia Avenue. I've seen the ownership papers when I was in his office and had to drop something off. He quickly covered it up and that's why I remembered. It's worth checking out, right?"

Clemente types another message on his phone and says, "I've put someone on it." His attention goes to Eddie as he says, "Can we talk in private?"

My first instinct is to leave them to it but then I realize they've been discussing details right in front of me and suddenly Clemente doesn't want me to hear what he has to say about Eddie? That means just one thing.

"He's mine and I'm his, Clemente," I snap. "Deal with it. I'm not giving him up because you can't handle the fact that we're together."

Clemente rises one eyebrow and says, "With the way you two interact, it's clear no one can come between the connection you share with him. My request to talk in private was indeed to split you up, but it was only for a short period of time because I don't want you near Spencer. Eddie and I will handle it so you'll either come with us and will be in another room, or—"

"She stays at the club," Rooney states. "She'll be surrounded by brothers who will protect her."

Yates nods and Eddie just gives a radiant smile.

Clemente sighs and says, "Fine. Just so we're clear, that's my sister. If anything happens to her, you're all going to wish you were dead, am I clear?"

"Dude." Rhett scrunches up his nose. "No need to throw out a threat like that. She's the president's old lady, your wrath would be peanuts compared to what Pres would do. Have you seen him fight? I was peeing blood for two days when he just lightly tapped my kidney the last time we were in the ring together. Yeah, no way would we let one hair on her head fall the wrong way, she's safe with us."

Eddie is still wearing the same smile when he gives me another kiss on my temple. "She stays at the club while I go with you."

Clemente lets his harsh gaze slide over Rooney, Yates, and Rhett, before he finally grunts, "Fine. But I'm coming back in to check if she's really fine when I drop Eddie off."

"Clemente!" I gasp, making the corner of his mouth twitch.

Eddie chuckles and slides his fingers to the back of my neck to pull me close as he takes my mouth. His tongue swoops in and swirls around mine. The kiss is hot, sensual, and he takes his time to claim my mouth for both our pleasure. Or he's just showing off to Clemente that I'm his to take care of. Either way, I don't mind because I'm reaping the benefits.

He rips his lips from mine and places his forehead against mine. "I won't be long. Stay with the guys and trust them if they make a decision concerning your safety, okay?"

I give him my word and leave the limo along with Rooney, Yates, and Rhett.

"Let's get you inside," Yates grunts. "I don't want you out in the open or near windows. The shit going on is insane."

Rooney places his hand at my lower back and guides me inside as the others follow.

"Let's see who Finn is humping," Rhett chuckles enthusiastically. "My money is on Hudson."

"I ain't betting with you, Rhett. You saw me hand over Finn to Hudson when Yates called us."

I turn and smack Rooney's arm. "That doesn't

mean he'll be humping Hudson."

"Wanna bet?" Rhett grins.

I roll my eyes. "No, I never bet. Besides, Finn humps everything, it's a no-brainer."

"Everything?" Rhett cringes.

My head bounces up and down. "Yup, everything he can wrap his front paw around and can bite down on."

"From now on, I'm locking my room," Rhett states as he dashes off toward the hallway, and I can't help but laugh.

"You want something to drink?" Yates offers.

I glance around and my eyes finally land on Yates. "I don't suppose you have wine since I'm only seeing beers in everyone's hands."

Hudson snickers as he sits down next to me. "You're right, but Eddie made us go out and buy supplies, including a crate of wine. Three to be exact because he wanted you to have a choice. So, what will it be? The only choice you have is white, red, or a rosé. Eddie already picked the brand, it's a good one, no worries there."

I glance at the clock and make my decision. "Make

it a rosé."

"You got it," Yates grunts.

Three glasses of rosé later and I'm really starting to know these guys. Not only do they work construction, Yates seems to own two apartments right next to each other and he lives in one while he's renting the other one to a woman.

The woman hasn't paid him for over three months and Rooney—the businessman he is—says he needs to give her a final notice and throw her out because she needs to pay. Hudson however suggested Yates makes her pay by giving his dick some attention. Naturally, I smacked Hudson on the back of his head and we ignored his suggestion.

Rhett returned before we had the discussion and he asked what reason the woman gave him. Turns out, she lost her job because her mother took a bad fall and she wanted to take care of her mother. That right there pulled on my heartstrings.

"I'll pay what she owes and the next two months too. That should give her a head start to look for a new job," I tell Yates.

He gives me a slow smile. "Nah, sweetheart. It's

fine. I already told her the same thing."

I reach out and pat his hand. "She's lucky you have a big heart."

"She and him could both be lucky because his dick is bigger than his heart," Hudson mutters.

And this time I can't help but laugh along with all the others. Finn is sleeping at my feet and this bunch is highly entertaining. They each have their own life and yet they spend the majority of their time either here or working. After a while we shift from the bar to the large round couch and Hudson turns on the TV and puts some series on the majority of the guys like and it makes time pass even quicker.

My eyes start to fall shut and when they open, I realize it's late at night and my head is leaning against Yates' shoulder. Eddie is standing in front of me and easily picks me up. I wrap my arm around his neck and cuddle close.

"I fell asleep," I mutter as he carries me to our room.

His chuckle rumbles through his chest. "I noticed."

"Yates is a sweetheart but not so good at the landlord thing," I mumble. "He lets his tenant live there for free while she finds herself a new job. But it's the whole taking life one wave at a time thing and how it echoes into the lives of others. She lost her job because she's taking care of her mother who had a bad fall. Yates lets her live there without the pressure of the money." I groan as Eddie places me on the bed. Maybe I had a little too much rosé. I can't remember what the point was I'm trying to make.

"Yates can afford it, no worries," Eddie says as he slowly strips me naked.

"I know, I offered to pay the woman's rent and he wouldn't let me."

Eddie chuckles. "You're both softhearted people. The whole heart at the right place when it matters."

"That's rare you know," I tell him and snuggle against the pillow as I crawl underneath the sheets. "There are a lot of rotten people in this world tainting the good ones."

"That's true," Eddie says as he spoons me from behind.

Skin to skin, that was fast. Shit. Finn. I dash up and glance around. "Where's Finn?"

"Sleeping in his bed in the corner. Now, let me hold

you so we can get some sleep. We're going to pick up my mother tomorrow. It's been a long day."

I snuggle back against him and sigh in contentment when I'm wrapped in his warmth. "You're right. And if I didn't drink too much rosé we would totally be having sex right now."

Another rumble of laughter vibrates through his chest. "Sleep, darlin'."

"Thanks for all the wine, I appreciate it," I mumble.

Right before I drift off to sleep, I hear him chuckle, "I noticed."

— CHAPTER THIRTEEN —

EDDIE

A soft hand slides over my abs and it feels so damn good, I don't want to open my eyes and ruin it. I want to keep relishing in the intimacy. Her lips trail a path down to where her fingers are now wrapped around my dick and suddenly, I do want to open my eyes when I feel her mouth covering the tip.

I take the blanket in hand and throw it back in one go, exposing Gracy sucking my dick and it's a beautiful sight. Her mouth goes up and down my length and it takes everything in me not to grab her head and thrust my hips up from the mattress.

But there's no need because her tiny head is bobbing, swallowing as she takes me deep while her hand is pumping up and down. My fingers travel up her back until they disappear into her hair, I fist it to keep her head in place.

I can't take it anymore, that mouth of hers is heaven's deadliest sin and it's burning so damn hot, it needs to be extinguished by my cum. My head tips back and a low groan rips from my body as I empty myself.

My heart is running like crazy and I have to take deep breaths to get all the air my body needs inside me. "Fuck, that was fantastic. Mind and cock blowing. I don't think I've ever started a day quite as fine as this."

She crawls up my body and places her cheek on my chest. I wrap my arms around her and keep her close. It takes a few minutes to catch my breath and relish in the way I feel complete to be in this bed with her. My old lady. Sunset, sunrise, the whole fucking universe complete with a future within our reach.

I hate thinking about the stuff Clemente and I took care of yesterday and yet it's a step forward in putting things behind us. The path to justice isn't always paved with shiny stones. It's a dirt road with bumps and holes but even if it's long and bumpy…it's the destination one longs for. And it's in sight and just the mere thought makes me smile. Not as bright and satisfying as holding this woman, I can tell you that.

Rolling over, I pin her underneath my body as I hover over her. "So. Fucking. Beautiful. And all mine," I whisper.

Her long black hair is sprawled out over the sheets, the morning sun highlighting the blueish glow. And when my eyes connect with hers it's an open window to her emotions. Fierce, welcoming, reaching out to entwine with mine.

"I've never felt with my whole being for a woman the way you connect with me." The words flow out naturally and without thinking.

The way her face changes with a reflection of the mirrored admiration we share for each other makes me aware what we have is real and only the beginning. I want to tell her so much more but it's too fast, too soon. So, instead I slide down her body, placing kisses as I go until I've reached the place I want to worship for a long time to come.

Glancing up, I see Gracy is on her elbows, biting

her lip with her eyes openly displaying the lust for what's to come. I keep our gaze connected as my tongue lazily slides from ass to clit and when my mouth completely covers that bundle of nerves and I start to flick it, that's when our connection breaks because her head tips back as a sexy moan falls from her lips.

Her taste is addictive and she completely surrenders to the pleasure I give her. Well, maybe not completely because both her hands slide into my hair and she starts to interfere by guiding my head exactly where she wants my tongue. She isn't shy in participating and those little instructions, "There…more…I need…yes!" followed by little mewls and moans are a real turn-on.

I gently shake my head to give her a nice stimulation with my scruff and that's when her taste intensifies. Her pussy starts to ripple as I spear her with my tongue. She screams my name as her juices flow freely. My dick is harder than ever and all I'm thinking about is burying myself deep.

Crawling up her body I thrust my tongue inside her mouth and simultaneously slide my dick deep inside her convulsing pussy. She gasps while her arms circle my body, her nails biting down in my skin. I'm not ashamed to call myself a madman at this point because my dick is pounding away as I'm trying to chase my orgasm that's almost within reach.

Bliss. Utter bliss is what the two of us create. I hook my arm around her leg to open her up some more and shift my hips for a slightly different angle. Fuck. Her nails trail a path up my spine and her pussy clamps down as if it's never going to let go. My dick surrenders and cum jets out in hard streams as if my whole body is fueling its energy.

I'm unable to keep my weight off her as I crash down onto her in utter exhaustion. There's a grunt and a light giggle breathing down my neck and I fucking relish in it. Shifting slightly, I take her with me as I turn.

My dick slides out of her pussy and it's then I realize, "Shit. No condom."

Her eyes grow wide. "We didn't use birth control."

I guide her head back to my chest. "Can we talk about this later? I'm still trying to catch my breath and I don't want to ruin the moment. Besides, we're in this together and the possibility of pregnancy is peanuts compared to the problems we've been facing since day one, don't you think?"

"I can't think," she squeaks. "And I can't believe you're this calm. Don't guys freak out over getting some girl pregnant?"

Now this grabs my attention and I give her a fierce look. "You're not some girl, Gracelynn. You're my woman. My old lady. My fucking future and that might entail kids down the line or not, a future isn't solid but we fucking are."

Her lips slightly part and a small, "Oh," slips past them.

"Yeah, oh," I grunt. "Now settle back down, we're doing the whole cuddle and afterglow shit."

A smile tugs her lips as she snuggles against my chest. Damn. I keep saying this, but she feels so good. And I need to relish in this moment together before I tell her what went down yesterday and what's going to happen in the days to come. I also need to decide if I give her the basics, tell her all, or remain silent. But that's also something to worry about later.

For now, it's the warmth and connection the both of us wrap ourselves with. And I have to say, the possibility of having a blood tie with this woman for life doesn't sound like a bad thing. I've never thought about kids but this woman makes me crave a lot of new things I'd like to explore with her beside me.

But, first things first. I thought I could enjoy a carefree moment but reality is knocking on our door and it's better to have her prepared. "I met your biological father yesterday."

She pushes herself up and is staring down at me. "You did?"

"Yeah, he wanted to be there when Clemente and I dealt with Spencer. He wants to meet with you again real soon too. Though, you know him but it's different now that the both of you know he's your father." I hope with this little piece of information she doesn't bother to question me about Spencer.

"Stephano wants to see me?" she whispers.

I let my knuckles brush her cheek. "Yeah, darlin', and he seemed quite anxious too. From what I heard and witnessed last night, the man loved your mother very much."

She places her head back on my chest and says,

"I wish things worked out differently for them. It would have made my life a whole lot different too, I'm sure."

"Never dwell on the past, Gracelynn. Even more now that we've found a future together. Positive stuff up ahead, and one thing at a time, that's how we're handling everything thrown in our path. Today we are going to pick up my mother. I'm going to make sure there's someone with her to take care of her."

"I could stay with her," Gracy says.

I kiss the top of her head and reluctantly say, "I wish I could stay with her too but there are things I need to deal with and for now she doesn't have a spotlight on her. Keeping her safe by not staying near her is our best option for now. A prospect and a brother will be in her bungalow at all times, while you're staying at my side."

"I have to swing by my boat later today. Can we fit that into your tight schedule?" she says mockingly.

I have her pinned underneath my body with my next breath. "If I can fit my dick into your tight pussy, everything else is smooth sailing."

She gasps when my dick rubs her clit. Feeling her

underneath me makes my dick spring to life for the third time today.

"Do you feel what you do to me? My body craves you so damn much it's ready for you at every turn."

She silences me with a kiss and the way she's clawing my back and wraps her legs around me, there are no words necessary to waste our thoughts on; our bodies are communicating quite nicely as it is.

Sliding home is a magical feeling. The thought of coming inside her pussy bare, knowing the risk of adding to our future is an enhanced exhilaration. And this time there's no place for raw and fast, it's intense and gentle. Between the pace of our heartbeats and the sexual tension is the difference between having sex and making love. The sex is there, our love is building, and our future is wide open for the taking.

But first we're taking our pleasure simultaneously and we are making sure to enjoy our time, to treasure the moment. Though, soon enough we have to leave the bed and hit the shower. We decide it's safer to take one separately because the mere thought of having her naked and available is making my dick hard and I've taken her pussy twice already.

No reason to make her so damn sore she won't be able to take me later tonight. Yeah, I'm not afraid to admit she's my new addiction. But like I said, we need to focus on the things we need to handle today. Though getting dressed while shooting heated glances at each other sure spices up my day.

"We're picking up Maggie, making sure she's settled in and then we're heading back here, or? What's the plan? Because I wasn't kidding when I mentioned I need to check on my boat," Gracy says as she picks up Finn and gives him a quick kiss.

I stroll over and pet him over the head. "Clemente is supposed to message me. There are things going down today we need to handle. I'm not even sure if it will be today or tomorrow, they still haven't been able to track down Rush so it all depends on when they find out where he's staying. I hate the uncertainty but it's unavoidable." I place a kiss on her forehead and grab my leather cut from the chair in the corner and put it on.

The room we're staying in is one of ten small rooms here at the clubhouse. There are about eight single brothers living here and the rest have their own house or apartment where they live.

My father used to live with my mother at the estate and I had both, a room here and a bungalow. The rooms here have just the basic necessities such as a king size bed, a chair along with a desk, a closet, and a separate bathroom. We all share the same kitchen.

There used to be a schedule of who cleans up the kitchen on what day, but I haven't seen any list, and the kitchen is a mess. So, I guess little things like that need my attention too. I make a mental note to discuss this in church. I have to smile at the minor necessary point of discussion and yet it's a way better thing to deal with than the shit we're wrapped in now.

The construction company my father owned was passed onto my mother and Yates has been keeping it afloat along with a few of the other brothers. Something else to discuss once things settle down, because eventually I will be back to working alongside my brothers.

My phone rings and when I check I see it's Clemente calling. "Yeah?"

"They found him...and the net is closing around Rush. I'm coming over in about two hours. I have a virtual meeting planned with my uncle in about twenty minutes, and I'm not sure how long it will take me to talk things through."

"Take your time, Clemente. We're heading out to bring my mother home. Shoot me a text when you're headed my way."

"Will do. Say hi to Gracy for me," Clemente says before he disconnects the call.

"Clemente says hi," I grumble and it makes Gracy smile.

Clemente's words echo through my mind and I now realize what he meant. Fuck. Spencer. We thought it would take them some time to find Spencer, I guess that ship sailed.

"Everything okay?" Gracy asks. "You seemed to mentally drift away to another place."

I shake my head. "It's nothing, come on, we're heading to the hospital and we're taking Finn with us. He can wait outside with Rhett while we're getting my mother. Then Finn can stay with her at her house so she'll have some extra company."

"You're right." Gracy starts to grab Finn's things. "She loves it when Finn is sitting next to her. Can't

Rooney come with us instead of Rhett? Or is Rhett staying with her today?"

"I haven't discussed it with Yates yet. I know most guys from way back but I've been away for a long time and don't exactly know their routine. Yates also handles the construction company where most of the guys work and as you know Rooney has his own company thrown into the mix too." I rub my jaw and think things through. "But I'm guessing it's Ash and either Rhett or Rooney. Maybe Hudson but I know he had three days off and he used to work one week nonstop and then have three days off and then a week nonstop again. He needs a routine in his life so I'm pretty sure he's unavailable."

"Your mother used to be an old lady, I'm pretty sure she can handle any biker you team her up with." She gives me a smile and says, "Ready when you are."

I hold the door for her and we head out to the main room in search of Yates. Turns out I was right about Hudson and Rooney. So, it's Rhett who is going with us while Yates needs to run out to a project that needs his attention. Yates assured me he'll be back within two hours if needed. We take the car as Rhett and Ash follow on their bikes behind us.

We're at the estate within the hour and I can clearly see my mother is glad she's home when she starts to cheerfully talk with Finn. I'm still worried, though. And I'm glad she agreed to a checkup in a few days because the papers she discovered might have set this off, but it's good to keep an eye on her health.

My mother grabs my arm and ushers me into the kitchen. There's a large safe in the pantry and she opens it and takes out her leather cut. She holds it out for me to take and when I do, I unfold it to check the back.

The two merged skulls with left and right, the rose and the dagger keeping everything pinned is in the middle while on top it says, "Property of," and on the bottom it states, "Barhamer."

"It shouldn't be kept in a safe, it should be passed on," my mother says, her voice filled with emotion.

"I wish he was here to see this moment," I grunt, not needing to mention my father's name because my mother knows damn sure who I'm talking about.

"It wasn't meant to be, son." She swallows hard and adds, "When the time comes, I will see him again, but for now he would want me to enjoy the sunset and sunrise while I know he's there with me in my heart."

"That's right, momma," I croak and pull her into a hug.

"Everything okay?" Gracy's worried voice flows through the kitchen.

"Oh, yes, child," my mother says as she walks over to Gracy and cups her face. "I knew you were special the day I met you. And it makes me very happy you two are together now. And remember, grandbabies. I'm not getting any younger."

"Ma!" I snap, exactly how I did at the hospital when she said the same thing, but at the same time satisfaction flows through my veins knowing there's a slight chance she might get her wish sooner rather than later.

My mother steps back and it allows me to hold out the leather cut for Gracy to see. Her fingers go to her lips and her eyes fill up. Her gaze meets my mother's and she nods approvingly, giving Gracy a tiny push so she moves to stand in front of me.

"Turn around," I grunt, my voice raw with the

loaded emotions.

My father gave his old lady this cut. He had it made special for everyone to see who my mother belonged to. Now, after all these years, it serves the same purpose for a new generation.

She slides her hands through the holes and puts it on. She turns and lets her fingers slide over the leather. Locking her gaze with mine she asks, "How do I look?"

"Fucking perfect and all mine," I tell her and take her mouth in a fierce but quick kiss.

She gives me a shy smile and wraps her arms around my waist to give me a hug.

"Okay, you youngsters, I'm going to grab a book and lie down on the patio with Finn keeping me company," mom says as she gives us both a smile and waves us out of the room.

By the emotions swirling in her eyes I can tell she's getting too emotional and needs to be by herself. I tell Rhett and Ash to keep an eye on her. Not just on the surroundings but on my mom as well to make sure she's okay.

When everything is set Gracy and I head back to

the clubhouse. It's time to take on another problem; Rush. One thing at a time is how we handle things, and our "to-do list" is getting shorter.

— CHAPTER FOURTEEN —

GRACY

Loud cheers cause me to stare at the floor all shy as my hands fiddle with the leather of the cut I'm wearing. A squeal rips from my throat when I'm being grabbed and lifted into the air.

"Look at that, pretty girl, you're officially off-limits with this cut showing everyone who you belong to," Yates bellows loud as he places my feet back on the floor.

"Then why are your fucking hands all over my woman?" Eddie growls and it makes me smile.

"Because she's ours to protect too, Pres," Yates

says and he smacks him on the back.

"Congrats man, babies are the next step, you know that, right? Knock her up so she's slow and easy to catch if she runs off."

Eddie grabs Yates' cut. "Knocked up or not, she's not running, not now, not ever."

"Overbearing weirdos," I mutter to myself and check my watch.

Normally I'd go to my boat a few times a week but if I won't be there for a long time, I make sure to double check everything and lock up properly. I'm positive I didn't double check and lock everything up the last time I left, when Eddie was with me. My mind was occupied with other things at the time. I'm not even sure if I locked up at all.

"When does Clemente get here? I really need to check my boat. Maybe I could go to and from the marina myself real quick. I'll be back within half an hour."

This gets me a stare from all the guys around me as if I'm the insane one.

"What?" I question.

"Rush is still out there, even if Clemente has eyes on him. You can't head out by yourself without protection," Eddie says and is now checking the time himself. "We will go together. I'm expecting him within half an hour so we would have to leave now and put a rush on it."

"Want me to tag along?" Yates asks.

"Nah, stay here and keep Clemente busy if he's early. We'll be right back," Eddie says as he places his hand on my lower back to usher me out of the club-house.

It's a quick ten-minute drive to the marina and when I step onto the boat I immediately feel something is off. The smell of gasoline enters my nose and I'm about to turn and tell Eddie, but a guy appears behind him, smacking him on his head with the butt of a gun and knocking him out as he crumbles onto the deck.

"Don't move," the guy grunts and I recognize him as Maxton, one of the guys who is working with Rush.

When Eddie was visiting Clemente, Rooney showed me pictures of all the guys and told me their names. He also mentioned Maxton, Banjo, and Den, pointing them out to me to make sure I'd stay away if I ever saw them. I guess it's too late now.

"Get off the boat, and no sudden moves," the other

guy standing next to him says and I recognize him as Banjo.

Are Den and Rush somewhere too? No, wait, didn't Eddie mention something about Clemente having eyes on Rush? My mind is trying to comprehend what's going on while all I can think about is Eddie, how hard did that asshole hit him? He passed out, that's bad, right?

"Move, cunt!" Maxton snaps and grabs me by my cut to drag me off the boat.

I try to kick and scream but Banjo places the gun against my forehead and says, "Maxton and Rush might think you're worth more alive, but make no mistake, I have a trigger-happy finger and would love to see you headbutt a bullet. Now calm down and be a good cunt. We're all going to take a little drive together."

"Not all of us, Banjo," Maxton chuckles and aims his gun toward my boat, fires once and makes the whole thing instantly blow up in flames.

"Nooooooo!" I scream with my whole heart.

This can't be happening. I just found the one person I want to spend the rest of my life with. There's no coming back from being in a sea of flames. My whole boat is gone. I couldn't care less about the boat, but Eddie is irreplaceable. I feel as if my heart was just ripped out of my chest and I can't breathe.

Another cry rips from my mouth and Maxton smacks a flat hand across my face, making me taste my own blood. I don't care about the blood or the taste. I don't even care if Banjo tries to make me headbutt a damn bullet, I want them to feel the pain coursing through my body.

Both assholes are smiling at the sky-high flames as I simultaneously kick Maxton and give Banjo a shove. Neither of them are expecting me to lash out as they stumble back. I try to think of what to do next when suddenly Eddie launches out from the water, grabs Maxton by his leg and takes him back into the water with him.

They disappear underneath the surface together. I rush over to see what's happening but Banjo grabs me, wraps his arm around my neck, and aims his gun at the place Eddie and Maxton just disappeared into.

He fires off two rounds and I elbow the idiot in the stomach. "Stop it, you could shoot either one, you idiot."

"I don't fucking care, it's Eddie. If he's still alive then Maxton is dead by now. Don't you fucking get it? It's the whole reason Rush put him in jail, because no one could get close enough to kill the fucker. His defense is always up at every turn, the asshole has eyes in his fucking back and can fight like a motherfucker."

There's a grunt and a snap and Banjo's body falls away from behind me. There's a splash and when I turn, I see Banjo's body disappear underneath the water. Eddie kicks the gun that fell onto the dock into the water and holds out his hand for me to take.

"We need to get out of here," he grunts, water dripping everywhere.

I don't think twice, grab his hand and follow him as he drags me to my car. He opens the trunk and kicks off his boots and throws them in the back along with his clothes until he's only wearing his boxers. I take out Finn's blanket I have on the backseat and give it a shake before folding it and placing it onto the passenger seat.

I get in behind the wheel and head for the clubhouse. There are no words exchanged but our fingers are laced and resting on my thigh. I need to feel him close, make sure he's still alive and here with me.

Yates comes rushing out of the clubhouse once we're opening the trunk. Eddie grabs his stuff and grumbles, "Don't fucking ask."

Yates looks stunned for a moment and glances at me, mouthing silently, "What happened?"

"Maxton and Banjo set my damn boat on fire and tried to kill Eddie along with it. They made a mistake, though, and it proves how brainless they are when even Banjo told me how Rush put Eddie in prison because no one could get close enough to kill him. But I guess we're lucky they're brainless because those idiots smacked him on the head with their gun instead of shooting him. They knocked Eddie out and then left him on the boat and set fire to it as they dragged me off. I mean seriously, if they know Eddie is the all-time greatest Unruly Defender...make sure he's dead or he'll make sure he's the last one to strike. You can't give that man an inch because as long as he's breathing, he will keep fighting for what he believes is the right thing to do," I tell Yates angrily.

"So, Maxton and Banjo are..." he trails off and raises his eyebrow at me in a request for me to finish the sentence.

"Swimming with the fishes," I snap. "Fish food. History. Another item crossed off the to-do list. Whatever."

I turn to head into the clubhouse but Eddie is standing in the doorway wearing a huge proud smile as he's watching me intently.

I put my hands on my hips and glare at him. "What are you smiling about? Go take a shower and put on some clothes because Clemente is coming over and we're not done handling things yet."

"My woman is bloodthirsty and I like it." Eddie grins.

I huff out a breath and murmur, "Well, you go and watch your boat being swallowed by flames, thinking the person you saw yourself spending the rest of your life with go up in a ball of fire instead, see how your state of mind can fart out sunshine and roses because all I can think of is getting even and wiping those fuckers off the face of the Earth."

Eddie slowly shakes his head. "My circumstances might have been different, and I've had a twisted timeout and walked back into this life with my mind set on revenge. Yet all I was thinking when I hit the water a few seconds before the boat was swallowed by flames was the fact that my only reason for living was you. I had to live and fight for you. Yes, justice needs to prevail, but fuck...not if it costs me my life or yours, Gracy. My heart might be beating on its own but you're the one holding it."

Yates whistles low. "That's some romantic shit right there. I need to remember that when I get myself an old lady."

"I hope I'll be there to ruin the moment like you're butting into ours," I growl.

Yates raises his eyebrows and glances at Eddie. "Your woman stays vicious when danger has been thrown her way."

"You have no idea," Eddie says proudly. "Now, as she ordered, I need a shower and a fresh set of clothes." He turns on his heels and heads into the clubhouse, leaving me and Yates to follow him.

Yates heads for the bar and pours me a glass of rosé and places it in front of me. "Here you go, sweets, you've earned it."

I don't even care what time it is, it's wine o'clock

in my book because I need it to take the edge off. Yates glances over my shoulder and walks away from the bar. I follow his movement and see he's opening the gates with a remote to let a limo inside. A moment later Clemente strolls into the clubhouse.

Yates smacks him on the back. "If there ever was any doubt, there's none now. Your sister here has the thirst for blood running through her veins and from the stuff I've heard? She's handling it like a damn pro. You should be fucking proud. Hell, I'm proud."

"What the hell happened?" Clemente snaps and he's standing in front of me before I can so much as blink. "Are you okay?"

"She's fine, a little shaken-up maybe, but she's strong," Eddie says as his arm sneaks around my waist from behind and places a kiss on the top of my head.

His freshly showered scent along with his after-shave—sandalwood and cinnamon, along with a hint of citrus—wrap around me, making me lean into his touch. I wish all of this was behind us so we could finally do some normal things like go out to dinner or a movie.

Clemente watches me with hawk eyes before they

slide back to Eddie. "Did you want to bring her along?"

"Everything is set? Handled? The part where you needed to contact your uncle about too?" Eddie questions.

Clemente winces and it's actually the first time I've seen him do this. I reach out and this time I'm the one who's asking, "Are you okay?"

"Other than the fact I'm suddenly engaged to be married, yes, all dandy." Clemente rubs a hand over his mouth before he drops it and his face is back to its familiar all business look. "A business deal, nothing I can't handle."

I feel my eyes widen. Did he just say? He can't be serious. "Are you telling me you struck a deal and your end was to marry some girl you don't even know? What the hell, Clemente? You can't be serious. Your own father didn't pressure you into this part of the family traditions. You know what happened to our father and my mother."

Clemente shrugs. "This is different. I don't do love and it was necessary. Besides, my uncle values the tradition and so do all others of the Famiglia. I'm the head of this Famiglia now Gracy, I can't ignore my responsibilities. Besides, from what I've heard she's supposed to be the beauty of Italy, she's going to look pretty on my arm."

"She's going to look…are you insane?" I screech and jab a finger against his chest. "Do I need to rip your brains out through your nose to check your sanity?"

His left eyebrow raises and his attention goes to Yates. "Thirst for blood and brains, eh?"

Yates grins. "She's an Unruly Defenders' old lady, you can't blame her for standing up for your future wife."

"You can pick her up from the airport in two weeks when she arrives. I was going to send the limo but maybe it's better if you—"

I cut him right off and huff, "You didn't just say that." I close my eyes for a brief moment and take a gulp of air to calm down. "Please don't tell me you're that guy. You know, the one who's a gloating, self-absorbed dick who is so damn impersonal that he sends a freaking limo to pick up his future wife to let her arrive all by herself to marry your insane, self-absorbed ass. Oh. My. God. Are we seriously related? Because if we are, we are going to have to spend a lot of time together so I can give you some proper advice on how to unjerk yourself, mister."

Laughter rings out around me and I have to shoot a glare around the clubhouse because this shit isn't funny. An arranged marriage? I can't begin to imagine what this woman might be thinking or what she's in for.

Clemente has always been sweet, kind, and caring to me but I've also seen the coldness his eyes can hold. And let's not forget the fact he's the head of the Famiglia. Talk about a lot of responsibility, stress, and a status to uphold.

"I agree to have you around me a lot more, Gracy," Clemente says, affection wrapping around each word. "It's why I suggested you pick her up at the airport but clearly I'm going with you. But I want her to feel welcome and I hope having you with me will put her at ease in some way."

"Nice save," I mutter and gulp down the rest of my rosé. "And what was that about bringing me along? To do what exactly?"

"Front row seat of Rush getting arrested for murder, among other things," Clemente casually throws out.

"Murder? He's finally going to get arrested for killing Eddie's father and his own? You guys leaked the evidence that implies he's behind all of it and how those men's death wasn't an accident at all?" Excitement fills my veins. Finally, there's light at the end of the tunnel to put an end to all of this.

Clemente is about to say something but Eddie's voice thunders from behind me, "Maybe it's best she stays here, and we need to be going, right?"

Clemente tilts his head slightly and I can see a nerve twitch underneath his left eye as he stares at Eddie. What's that about?

"We're going, but she's coming with us," Clemente states.

"I don't think that's a good idea," Eddie starts.

"It's not up to you, it's my decision. She's my sister and I'm telling you she's coming with us."

Okay, then. I guess I'm about to find out what's going to happen next.

— CHAPTER FIFTEEN —

EDDIE

I'm not liking this one damn bit. I glance to my left and watch how Gracy is looking out the window, her hands folded and resting on her lap. I wanted to save her from this part and I know it's wrong but it's going to be like pouring salt on already open wounds.

I reach out and take her hand in mine. She instantly leans her body in my direction and I relish in the way we've grown close in such a short period of time. The limo comes to a stop and I give her hand one last squeeze to get her attention.

"Whatever is said inside, I know it's going to be

hard for you to hear and understand. But you need to know I'm right here for you, and there are a lot of others around you who also love you and are there for anything you need, okay?"

Her eyes stare into mine and are checking to see if there's an answer for the unspoken thoughts I just gave her. Until mischief starts to dance in her eyes.

"Also love me," she muses. "Eddie, is this your sneaky way of saying you love me?"

A smile spreads my face, making my cheeks hurt, and I shake my head. "Woman, I'm trying to tell you to brace yourself and all you catch is the love you part?"

She shrugs but I can tell by the flush of her cheeks and the way her gaze hits her lap that she's feeling vulnerable and this is turning less into a casual discussion or joke.

I place my finger underneath her chin and tip her head up so she can look at me while I give her my words. "We might have just started but the connection we share was locked like a solid unbreakable chain. Whatever the chain is made of, steel, silver, gold, platinum? Does it represent value? Not to me because it's the meaning behind it that counts, not the name you attach to it. So, adoration, love, head over heels, or the feeling of belonging together…one, the other…it's all about the feelings expressed between us. And what I feel for you in this moment in time is solid, and I can also tell you it will only become fiercer and stronger. I'm not giving you the exact words right now, but I am warning you...do not walk away from me at any time, because you're the one holding my heart, Gracelynn."

Her eyes go wide at my admittance but Clemente breaks our connection when he grunts, "This is why I don't do the whole love thing. It makes me physically nauseous."

Gracy glares at him and snaps, "You reap what you sow. You'd do best to open up some or you'll end up with an ice queen for a wife."

Clemente shrugs. "I don't see any problems with it. As long as she melts between the sheets."

"For fuck's sake," Gracy mutters and shakes her head disapprovingly.

"Showtime, folks," Clemente says and the door of the limo opens.

Just before we head inside, I lean in and whisper right next to Gracy's ear, "Remember, you have a whole new family at your back."

She turns and surprises me by grabbing my head and crashing our lips together for a fierce kiss.

When she pulls back she says, "Sunrise, sunset, and everything in between."

"Everything in between," I croak.

"Then let's do this," she says fiercely and laces her fingers with mine.

The moment we step inside tension thickens the air around us. Clemente checks his gold watch and I know he must have more information than he shared with me. This man has contacts everywhere and can make anything happen. He doesn't even need the added bodyguards surrounding him because everywhere he goes people know what he represents and the repercussions along with it if something were to happen to him.

The sound of someone stumbling comes from our right and Rush comes around the corner. His face shows lacerations and bruises and his eye is swollen shut. He pulls a gun on us and I roughly shove Gracy behind me.

Clemente is aiming his gun at Rush's head and releases a humorless chuckle. "Put it away, asshole.

You're a dead man walking as it is, and no one in here is going to join your trip to hell. And it has nothing to do with the beating you took. But, in case you were wondering, I'm delighted to tell you I'm the one you can thank for the little postponement of your nearing death. You little, pitiful speck of a man. Did you really think you could get away with setting up shop in my district without me knowing or agreeing? Not to mention what you did to my family. This has been a long time coming but you'll know soon enough. I deliberately ordered the cartel to keep you breathing when they gave you the beating and handled Den since he was of no use to me but you? I have plans for you. Plans that involve justice on a different kind of level since my sister deserves it. And seeing she's the old lady of the man you sent to prison for shit he didn't do, he deserves his chunk of justice too."

Sirens start to flare up in the distance.

"Ah, right on time," I grunt, already knowing what's to come.

"They can't touch me. I didn't do shit," Rush grunts.

Clemente slowly shakes his head. "On the

contrary, Rush, we know exactly what you did. And everyone else will know soon enough too."

The sirens are becoming louder and Rush locks his eyes on me. "This will play out the same way it did when they came for me back at the clubhouse. I'm walking out within a few hours. You have nothing on me."

"Spencer won't bail you out this time, Rush," I state, feeling Gracy tense behind me.

The police burst inside and I notice Clemente isn't holding his gun anymore. Rush is the only one holding one and with the loud shouting and guns pointing from the law, Rush surrenders and finds himself with his hands cuffed behind his back. They read him his rights and when they mention the reason, I hear Gracy gasp behind me.

Her tiny fists clench around my leather cut and in this moment I'm glad Clemente has the right connections because we're allowed to slip away from the scene as I guide her outside. It's time I shared this final piece of information with her because I don't want any secrets between us and with the recent events it's clear she can handle a lot.

Though this part will hit hard and I'm trying to think of a way to start but she catches me by surprise when she whispers, "When you went with Clemente to handle Spencer...you made it seem Rush did it?"

I wince at the way she easily supplies we killed a man and voices it as "handle it."

"Not exactly. We did have a long talk with him but it was mostly Clemente's father, Stephano...your father...who did the talking...and the handling part. But, Gracy," I croak and I place my hands on her hips to keep her pinned. "When Stephano pressured Spencer, Spencer admitted something Clemente and Stephano already suspected."

She swallows hard and the way a tear slides down her face, it's not hard to guess she knows what I'm about to say.

"Spencer paid Rush to kill your mother and made it look like a suicide. A few days before her death, your mother contacted a lawyer and had divorce papers drawn up. She was officially going to leave Spencer. He would be left with nothing. Not one penny. This was the reason he needed her gone and also filed the papers to have you give up the inheritance so he could get his hands on everything. I'm very thankful you walked out of his life all those months ago because I have a feeling this man wouldn't have thought twice to get rid of you too."

I pull her close and I feel her arms sliding around my waist to hold me just as tight.

Clemente stalks up and asks, "Everything okay?"

Gracy pulls back and croaks, "I don't think it's going to be okay for a while. But with the support of those around us we will pull through, right?"

Clemente opens his arms and Gracy turns to accept his hug. "Right," he murmurs and places a kiss on the top of her head.

He eyes me for a moment and the slight lift of his chin lets me know I made the right decision. I would have wanted nothing more than to kill Rush with my bare hands but it was too much of a risk. Not to mention we needed him to take the fall for the shit he did so everything is out in the open and all of us will get the closure we need.

This is why I talked Clemente into getting the police involved and making sure he's thrown in jail to pay for the crimes he did. Satisfaction roars in my veins when I see them drive Rush off. Closure. Justice finally wraps around all of us and it's the first step in putting everything behind us.

Open wounds will take a while to heal, but with the right gentleness and care, there isn't anything we can't handle together. Because when I look at Gracy, I see my future and the brightness of the sun that holds all the warmth my heart is filled with.

All of us get into the limo and ride back to the clubhouse. Clemente and Gracy agree to have dinner next week along with her father and though I didn't want to intrude, the both of them made sure I said yes to joining them.

It's hard to believe I'm stepping into the clubhouse with the knowledge everything is handled. I know there are a lot of things to do but I feel lighter now that we don't have to glance over our shoulder at every turn.

Building the future is what needs our attention and it's exactly where my devotion is. To build this club stronger than it was. To run my father's company with the same dedication he once started it with. And to spend as much time in my mother's presence…and finally, to make sure I enjoy every sunset and sun-rise with the woman who holds my heart.

And when I glance down and lock eyes with her, I can see the same promise reflecting in her eyes. Time is precious and while each of us have the one life we're living, you have to make damn sure to set priorities and make the right choices about how much everything is worth to you in the end.

I might have been consumed with the need for vengeance, blinded by it so much I was willing to risk my own life along with it. Instead I'm glad to say, somewhere along the line, it shifted by the more im-portant things life has to offer. And in the end, it all worked out the way it's supposed to be, with one huge difference…my bright as fuck future I intend to enjoy every damn second of.

Like I said, it's all behind us and when Yates hands me a cold beer and Gracy a glass of rosé, we share an-other look. Though mine is one where I take her glass out of her hands and give it back to Yates.

"You're not allowed to drink," I tell her and her eyes go wide at my demand.

She starts to sputter but stops when I point at her

belly. Her lips part as understanding dawns. Her shoulders sag and she grumbles, "Then you'd better entertain me in another way because I'm allowed to have a little stress relief to make my body fill with joy."

A growl rumbles low in my chest as I thrust the beer back into Yates' hands. "I'll give you plenty of entertainment all right." I grab her by the waist and hoist her onto my shoulder, heading for my room the next instant as I smack her ass and tell her, "Fill your body up with joy...cum-ming right up."

"Dirty man," Gracy squeals as her giggles trail through the air behind us.

"We're having a party, kids," Yates bellows. "You can't skip your own late 'welcome home, slash, we finally settled that shit' celebration party."

"The day is still young, Yates," I shout back before I open the door to our room.

There's no way I'm missing out on making love with my woman. I'm pressing pause on the whole damn world because there's nothing more important than sharing an intimate moment with the one you love. The one who opened my eyes and took my hand to guide me into the part where life becomes worth living.

—— THREE WEEKS LATER ——

"I don't know if I can do this," Gracy whispers as we're standing in front of a large mansion that's owned by her biological father.

I step in front of her and cup her face. "You've been postponing this for three weeks now. It's time. Besides, you already met him a few times before you knew he was your biological father. You've mentioned how friendly and sweet he was and how your mother loved spending time with him. There's no need to be nervous. Clemente is here, you've seen him multiple times after knowing he's your brother. And I'm right here too."

"I know I've seen Clemente, but it's not like he killed Spencer. I can't help but be afraid I will blurt out something about Spencer and rattle off words how I think he should have come back for me and how my mother should have told him about me the second she knew she was pregnant. See? I'm such a mess with all of this." Her voice cracks up at the end and I know how hard these past weeks have been for her.

She might have been holding up strong but when the dust settles it's the pieces you have to pick up behind you to move forward. We've been doing this together but Gracy has been putting this meeting off for weeks now and it's not helping either one.

Clemente has called me a few times to ask for my help in bringing them together because his father has been doing better ever since he killed Spencer. He's excited to meet Gracy and I can't blame him, everyone loves her.

All the bikers of Unruly Defenders MC love her and go out of their way to make her feel at home at the clubhouse. And that's another thing, she demanded we'd live at the clubhouse for the time being.

It was something I would have been willing to compromise with because the estate is close by too, but I loved her reasoning since it mirrored my own. The MC needs me—and her along with it—as a visible presence. Building up everything just as the connection between us. The strong foundation is there and we have all the time in the world to make it stronger to rise above.

"We're all family, Gracelynn. And some might think we're a screwed up one, but we relish in that shit because at our dinner table there isn't a limitation of what can or cannot be discussed. So, you throw out what's on your mind. I'm pretty damn sure your father would rather face awkward questions than to not see you at all."

Her eyes fill with understanding and determination. "You're right. We're doing this."

"We are," I agree and ring the bell before she can change her mind.

It's unnecessary to ring the bell because we already passed security but I'm sure they were watching the cameras and gave us this moment before opening the door.

My suspicion is correct when Clemente is the one opening the door. "Sis, glad you could make it."

"And I'm glad to see you're still alive," Gracy mutters before she shoots him a vicious grin and asks, "How's your fiancée doing?"

There isn't a twitch on his face as he instantly

replies, "Still breathing and plotting ways to kill me, the usual."

The corner of my mouth twitches. The deal he made through his uncle to make the cartel Rush was working with back off, is backfiring because the woman he needs to marry turns out to be a temperamental spitfire and quite his match.

Gracy was there when he needed to pick her up from the airport and has been visiting her regularly. As a result, they have started to build up a friendship. Clemente doesn't even seem phased by the fact Gracy takes his fiancée's side most of the time when it comes to any argument thrown between them. He's actually happy those two hit it off as friends.

"Give her my best," Gracy chuckles and I follow her into the hallway.

Clemente leads us to a large room with a fireplace. The rest of the space is breathtaking but the fireplace is huge. Large enough to burn a body instead of some wood chunks. I rip my eyes away from it and glance around.

Two large couches are placed across from each other with a table in between with a fluffy white rug draped over the granite floor. The ceiling is high and so are the floor to ceiling windows on one side of this space. I count two big green plants and nothing on the wall. It's a modern interior and yet it radiates no warmth.

"Gracy, Eddie," Stephano's baritone voice rumbles as he steps closer and holds out his hand for me to take.

"Sir." I nod and shake his hand.

His attention shifts to my woman, his daughter.

"Gracy," Stephano says again and takes her hand in both of his. "I'm glad you could come."

"And I'm glad you killed Spencer." She gasps at her own words and releases a string of curses as she pulls her hand away from Stephano.

Gracy's head swings to me and she's wearing a look that states, "I told you this would happen."

"I'm glad you feel that way." Stephano releases an uneasy chuckle and points at the couch. "Why don't we have a seat and have a little talk, it's way overdue, don't you think?"

Gracy smiles at him and follows Stephano to the couch. I'm about to do the same but Clemente stops me. "Eddie, can I have a word?"

I glance at Gracy but she's already wrapped in a discussion with Stephano and when I see him handing over a pile of pictures of her mother in her younger years, I know these two need to have a private talk. Clemente and I slip out of the room and head for the garden.

"Did you drag me out here to give those two some space? If so, I could use a cold beer."

Clemente shoots me a grin and takes out his phone and types away. It doesn't take long for a guy in a suit to stroll out, a bottle of Heineken in each hand. There's a moment of silence where we watch the guy leave and just sit to enjoy the sun beaming down on us.

"Rush is handled, I thought you needed to know," Clemente suddenly says.

My head whips in his direction. "Handled?" I question, wondering just what he means by this because Rush was handled; rotting in jail for the rest of his life.

"Remember the deal I made with my uncle when I reached out so the cartel would disappear from this district? It included for them to clean up loose ends. Rush died in a prison riot yesterday, we just received confirmation."

All I can do is stare at Clemente. He takes a slow sip and gives me a wry smile. "You didn't think we were going to allow the chance of him escaping and coming anywhere near Gracy, did you? He killed her mother, Eddie."

I slowly shake my head, understanding his reasoning but also aware how his life and mine are worlds apart. His ways are ruthless whereas I was seeking justice. And yes, my thoughts might have gone to the place where I wanted to kill Rush with my bare hands but I'm also aware of consequences. I guess Clemente and his father don't have those problems.

I take a pull from the cold beer and almost spit it out when Clemente says, "I need your advice on how to handle a woman because I'm not going to survive handling the one I'm saddled up with."

Motherfucker, how does this guy easily change topics like this, and for fucking real, "Are you seriously asking me this? You, a man who practically runs the underworld of California, can't handle one single woman?"

"I could," Clemente grunts. "But that would mean I have to follow into Famiglia tradition I don't want to dabble in. There's a difference in control, Eddie. You of all people should know what the MC is like when it's being led by you or when it was swallowed by the dictatorship of Rush. You have the men's respect while they had none for Rush. And it's not that I want her to respect me, but a form of being equal would be nice."

I think of how to answer his question. "There is no simple answer, Clemente. The two of you need to find a way to come together. If you're going head to head together this fierce it shows raw emotion. The whole fine line of love and hate." I swallow another sip of my beer and tell him, "First time I met Gracy it didn't exactly go smoothly. We were snapping and grunting at each other. I'm telling you this because a connection can be instantly and might have to settle before it can be exploited. Who knows, the way you flare up and go head to head with each other…it might lead to fireworks between the sheets."

Clemente stares hypnotized at his beer until he drags his gaze away and mutters, "Who knows." His head swings my way. "We'll find out next week since our wedding day is set. How about you and my sister?

Any plans on getting married?"

"Way to shift the attention from you to me, ass-hole." A bark of laughter slips past my lips and flows away as his question roams around in my head. "To be honest…if I knew she'd say yes, I'd drop to one knee and pop the question right fucking now. There might be a lot of uncertainty in life but she's the one thing solid, she's mine."

"It would have been nice if you'd ask my permission first," Stephano grumbles from behind us, making me turn to stare in the watery eyes of the woman who will always hold my heart.

"Then you'd better get on one knee and pop that question because my answer would be yes," she croaks, giving me her heart to hold in return.

—— EPILOGUE ——

GRACY

Seven years later

A third. I can't believe I'm staring at another stick with lines. Eddie is going to be thrilled while I need to blink a few times to process the fact I'm pregnant for the third time. Growing up I was an only child, Eddie too. Ever since I became aware I have a brother, we've grown close and I have to admit, our bond is special.

Clemente was overly excited when he heard he was going to be an uncle. It's where Eddie is dropping our two sons off now for a day of being spoiled by my side of the family. Our oldest son, William—named after Eddie's father—is six years old. Our youngest, Lucas, is four. Well, I guess he's not our youngest anymore because the tiny life of eight weeks old has claimed that title.

To think today is our anniversary. Seven years ago, he asked me to marry him just a few weeks after we met. Some might have thought it would have never last but we knew our connection was deep and real.

We didn't even need a lot of time in between and had a small wedding at the clubhouse with all the bikers. Eddie's mother was there, Travis, my father, Clemente and his wife. And Eddie's friends, Chance Bateman and Aubrey Bloom. Though they have become my friends too over the years and we frequently visit each other.

My hand lets go of the stick I just peed on and I wash my hands while staring at my reflection in the mirror. Maybe this time it will be a girl. Maybe another boy to add to the soccer team Eddie has in mind. I'm not kidding, the man wants a truckload of kids but as we mentioned in the weeks we started our life together…one thing at a time. Which translates now to one kid at a time.

I head downstairs and mentally check what I have

to eat in this house. When we found out I was pregnant, Eddie wanted to add to his mother's bungalow. We all loved the idea and he talked it through with the architect of Maggie's construction company and together with Yates they made a plan and set things in motion.

Eddie added a few spare bedrooms along with a special bedroom downstairs with an extended bathroom for Maggie. She's not getting any younger, though the way she enjoys spending time with her grandkids says otherwise, because she can entertain them for hours. This little fact makes me question where she gets the energy from since some days, I'm completely exhausted.

Between running the estate and the kids, there's little time to put my feet up and do nothing. But I guess when I find the time to sit on the patio with a kid on each side while Eddie is sitting next to me, Maggie on the other side and Finn sleeping at our feet…it makes everything worthwhile.

And when you think of the extra special moments where we all sit and stare at how the sun kisses the water goodnight as we cuddle our kids close. Who dares to complain about hard work while you get so much in return for the life you live?

There's a balance in our life where we all reap the benefits. The construction company is still in Maggie's name while Eddie and Yates are the ones who run it. The estate is in Eddie's name though I'm the one running it most days while Travis, and all the other personnel do their part too.

The MC is where we spend a lot of time and like I said, there's a balance. Eddie and I have our date night once a week where we most times end up in the clubhouse relaxing with the guys while they enjoy a beer and serve me wine. We have careless chitchat and I'm thankful we haven't run into any dangerous things our life together started out with.

Though, I have a feeling it also has something to do with my father and Clemente. Those two might have thrown out a memo that stated "Touch her and die" because even Yates has mentioned it to Eddie how smooth sailing these years have been compared to all the previous years they were in this MC.

I glance at the list of groceries I need to pick up and smile at the little doodles on the bottom. I'm pretty sure Lucas added something for himself on the list and it warms my heart when the memory hits me of my mother. I used to do the same thing…add stuff like cookies and chocolate.

I can feel a tear slide down my face but it's not the sadness that overtakes me, it's the loving memory I keep alive because she touched my life in ways she'll always be connected with me. If only she could see me now. Also a mother and yet again my belly is filled with the promise of new life.

"You're crying?" Eddie grunts as he stalks into the kitchen, his hands cupping my face the next instant. "Why?" he demands while his thumbs brush away the wetness on my cheeks.

"Lucas added to my grocery list and it made me think of my mother…sweet memories," I croak.

"Her blood is running through you, and through our kids, she's still here with us, darlin'," he murmurs and pulls me against his comforting chest.

"I know," I whisper and wrap my hands around his waist. "I'm just a bit emotional with all those pregnancy hormones running through me."

His whole body goes tight for a second before I'm

being ripped away from his body. Two strong hands are holding me at arm's length to allow him to lean in and press his nose to mine. "Did you just…are you saying? Pregnant?"

His eyes hold all the love I have for this man as I give him what he's desperately wanting to hear. "Yes, Eddie, you've managed to knock me up again."

"Fuck, yes," he bellows and hoists me up against his body and starts to spin me around.

He lets me slide down and takes my mouth in a ravishing kiss. His tongue dominates mine as my hands slide into his hair, my nails teasing his scalp to egg him on. Eddie grabs my ass and places me on the counter, mindlessly shoving up my summer dress until his hands still on the garter belt I'm wearing.

I know he's obsessed with them, even more than I am so it feeds both our addictions and I have a drawer in the bedroom that's overflowing with sexy lingerie. Ever since Eddie came into my life the meaning of wearing lace shifted from putting it on to make me feel good to making the both of us feel good.

During the day it breaks our everyday life when he runs a hand down my hip in an effort to find out what

I'm wearing underneath. Boy shorts, thong, or garters like now? Though the last one I always save for special occasions, to really spice things up.

He steps away and gently slides the dress up to see what's underneath. His sharp intake of breath indicates he's loving the new deep red set I bought the other day. Gripping the hem of my dress, I rip it off over my head and let if fall onto the kitchen floor.

The way Eddie looks at me—like a starving man with a dinner table filled with delicious food right in front of him—is all consuming. He gently pushes me back by my shoulders and grabs my legs to pull me slightly forward and with it put my ass and pussy on the ledge as he bends down to place his head between my legs.

His nose trails a path over my pussy as he inhales deep. A low approving growl rips from his chest and is making my heart skip a beat. I know what's coming and I'm biting my bottom lip in anticipation.

My thong is ripped to shreds right before his tongue slides through the lips of my pussy. I want to watch so bad but the pleasure is making my head tip back while a low moan escapes me. This is what my man does to me, an instant connection where we're both con-sumed with the pleasure we create and share together.

His teeth graze my clit and I know my orgasm is hovering at the surface. Slow and lazy licks turn to a frenzy soon enough as he shakes his head roughly as if he's devouring my pussy completely. The extra stimu-lation of his scruff and the way he's sucking my clit is too much of a sensatory overload and I gladly sur-render to the waves of pleasure coursing through my body.

I'm still releasing a low moan when Eddie lifts his head and wipes his mouth with the back of his hand, satisfaction tainting his features. "My turn," he says gruffly and lifts me up from the counter and places me on my feet before he spins me around.

"Hands on the counter and hold tight, darlin'," he says in a way too sexy tone, making my pussy clench with anticipation.

I'm not expecting the smack on my ass, making the kitchen fill with the sound of my yelp and Eddie's chuckle right after.

"My red handprint makes it complete," he mutters to himself as I can feel him knead my ass cheeks.

I glance over my shoulder and see how his gaze is set between my legs. Hypnotized. He's completely enthralled and breathing heavily. I have to swallow at the emotions going through me. This man is my everything. The one who is there for me, for our children, for his mother, for the companies we run and the life we lead.

His head comes up and his gaze collides with mine. "Fuckin' love you," he grunts, his eyes going down to my pussy again.

"Fuckin' love you too," I murmur back and it makes a slow satisfied grin spread his face.

The sound of a zipper bites through the air and it's the moment my eyes fall shut and my hands grip the counter to steady myself as he fills me up in slow, consuming thrusts. His hand slides up my spine until he's gripping my shoulder to keep me pinned, his other hand locked on my hip as he starts to pound inside me.

The heat of his body covers me completely as he leans down and puts his mouth right next to my ear, grunting words on a hot breath to make my pussy clench in appreciation. Loving words. Dirty words. Words that shouldn't be voiced out loud but are reserved for two people who after all these years found a way to increase their love with each day passing.

I feel his thrusts start to falter and his grunts intensify. "Come for me, Gracelynn."

Guttural. Demanding. And yet oh so loving. I can only surrender and as always he's right behind me. My orgasm hits the same moment his dick inside me starts to pulse. Electricity bounces off our skin while the both of us are surrendering to be consumed with pleasure.

In this moment time seems to freeze and it's where your mind doesn't process anything other than ecstasy. Mind and body melting with the kind of euphoria that's shared between two people who connect flawlessly.

It takes a few breaths to come down from our shared bliss and I reach my arm back to touch his head. Sliding further back, my fingers slide over fabric and I now notice he's still wearing his shirt. A giggle slips past my lips when I realize he didn't even take off his clothes.

"What?" Eddie grunts against the skin of my neck.

"You only unzipped yourself, didn't you?" Laughter is wrapped around each word.

Eddie pulls back and stares down at me, a smirk sliding over his handsome face. "I was in a hurry, can you blame me? Damn, red garters," he says, and I can feel his dick twitch inside me, sliding out the next instant, making the both of us groan.

He reaches out to grab a clean cloth from the cabinet and holds it between my legs. It makes me snicker and say, "I'm already pregnant, Eddie, no need to stop your cum from leaking out."

His face turns serious. "I'm hoping for twins this time."

My eyes go wide and his head tips back as laughter rips out. I step away from the counter and when I start to shoot him a witty reply, I'm robbed from doing so by the sound of a squeaky toy.

My heart is beating in my throat and for a split second I try to think where the kids are. By the way Eddie's eyes are growing wide I'm guessing he's thinking the same thing. That is until he glances around me and snickers.

Turning, I see what made the noise and watch how Finn is humping a rubber chicken. Loud laughter escapes the both of us as Eddie pulls me into his arms and holds me close. This is our life.

It might not be perfect and filled with stress, work, kids, and all kinds of bumps in the road…but we take one thing at a time and enjoy the tiny moments that capture the love and laughter one can live off forever.

"Come on, let's get you dressed before I have to defend your honor against a rubber chicken," Eddie chuckles as he kisses the top of my head.

I step out of his loving arms and pat his shoulder. "No challenge too big for my Unruly Defender." I turn to head for the bathroom and glance over my shoulder as I say, "But I'm pretty sure you couldn't handle that rubber chicken."

There's a loud growl ripping from him and when he takes one step, I know it's time for me to run. A squeal rips through the air when he catches me from behind, throws me over his shoulder and stalks right into the bedroom as he smacks my ass.

"I'll show you just how much I can handle," he rumbles.

My mind says "Yes, please," in sync with my pussy while my heart already knows he can handle anything life throws our way.

UNRULY DEFENDERS MC

Thank you for reading Unruly Defender's story. Gaining exposure as an independent author relies mostly on word-of-mouth, so if you have the time and inclination, please consider leaving a short review wherever you can. Even a short message on social media would be greatly appreciated.

Want to keep up with all of the new releases in Vi Keeland and Penelope Ward's Cocky Hero Club world? Make sure you sign up for the official Cocky Hero Club newsletter for all the latest on our upcoming books: ***subscribepage.com/CockyHeroClub***

Check out other books in the Cocky Hero Club series: ***www.cockyheroclub.com***

UNRULY DEFENDERS MC

— SPECIAL THANKS —

My beta team;
Neringa, Tracy, my bestie Christi,
my editor Virginia Tesi Carey,
and to you, as my reader…
Thanks so much! You guys rock!

UNRULY DEFENDERS MC

Contact:

I love hearing from my readers.

Email:

authoresthereschmidt@gmail.com

Or contact my PA **Christi Durbin**
for any questions you might have.
facebook.com/CMDurbin

Visit Esther E. Schmidt online:

Website:

www.esthereschmidt.nl

Facebook - AuthorEstherESchmidt

Twitter - @esthereschmidt

Instagram - @esthereschmidt

Pinterest - @esthereschmidt

Signup for Esther's newsletter:

esthereschmidt.nl/newsletter

Join Esther's fan group on Facebook:

www.facebook.com/groups/estherselite

— MORE BOOKS BY —
ESTHER E. SCHMIDT

UNRULY DEFENDERS MC

UNRULY DEFENDERS MC

UNRULY DEFENDERS MC

UNRULY DEFENDERS MC

MC
LOST VALKYRIES

UNRULY DEFENDERS MC

UNRULY DEFENDERS MC

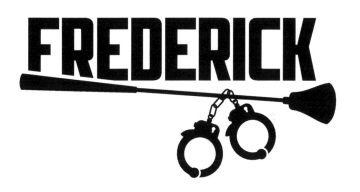

UNRULY DEFENDERS MC

UNRULY DEFENDERS MC

PEACOCK

THE FAULTS OF OUR SINS

UNRULY DEFENDERS MC

Manufactured by Amazon.ca
Bolton, ON